UTOPIA

UTOPIA

Thomas More

a *Broadview Anthology of British Literature* edition

General Editors,
Broadview Anthology of British Literature:
Joseph Black, University of Massachusetts, Amherst
Leonard Conolly, Trent University
Kate Flint, Rutgers University
Isobel Grundy, University of Alberta
Don LePan, Broadview Press
Roy Liuzza, University of Tennessee
Jerome J. McGann, University of Virginia
Anne Lake Prescott, Barnard College
Barry V. Qualls, Rutgers University
Claire Waters, University of California, Davis

Contributing Editor, *Utopia*:
William P. Weaver, Baylor University

broadview press

Library and Archives Canada Cataloguing in Publication

More, Thomas, Sir, Saint, 1478-1535
     Utopia / Thomas More ; edited by William P. Weaver.

Translated from the Latin.
Includes bibliographical references.
ISBN 978-1-55111-966-3

     1. Utopias—Early works to 1800.
I. Weaver, William P II. Title.

HX810.5.E54 2009   335'.02   C2009-905448-5

Broadview Press is an independent, international publishing house, incorporated in 1985.

We welcome comments and suggestions regarding any aspect of our publications—please feel free to contact us at the addresses below or at broadview@broadviewpress.com.

North America	PO Box 1243, Peterborough, Ontario, Canada K9J 7H5
	2215 Kenmore Ave., Buffalo, New York, USA 14207
	Tel: (705) 743-8990; Fax: (705) 743-8353
	email: customerservice@broadviewpress.com
UK, Europe, Central Asia,	Eurospan Group, 3 Henrietta St., London WC2E 8LU, UK
Middle East, Africa, India,	Tel: 44 (0) 1767 604972; Fax: 44 (0) 1767 601640
and Southeast Asia	email: eurospan@turpin-distribution.com
Australia and New Zealand	NewSouth Books, c/o TL Distribution
	15-23 Helles Ave., Moorebank, NSW, Australia 2170
	Tel: (02) 8778 9999; Fax: (02) 8778 9944
	email: orders@tldistribution.com.au

www.broadviewpress.com

Broadview Press acknowledges the financial support of the Government of Canada through the Canada Book Fund for our publishing activities.

Developmental Editor: Jennifer McCue
Editorial Assistant, In Context Materials: Laura Buzzard

This book is printed on paper containing 100% post-consumer fibre.

PRINTED IN CANADA

Contents

Introduction

Thomas More was one of the most impressive figures of the English Renaissance. His writings on politics, religion, faith, and history, his translations of Lucian from the Greek, and his witty Latin epigrams, together with his activities as lawyer, parliamentarian, and Lord Chancellor, won him international fame as an author, a vigorous polemicist, an influential statesman, and, eventually, a Catholic martyr. He is remembered above all for his *Utopia*, an important work of satirical political speculation, and for maintaining his principles during one of the nastiest political struggles in English history—a moral choice that cost him his life.

More was born in London on 7 February 1478, the son of Agnes and Sir John More, a lawyer and judge. As a boy, he studied at St. Anthony's School in London before leaving at age 13 to become a page in the household of John Morton, Archbishop of Canterbury and a future cardinal. Morton recognized More as a promising, intelligent boy, and had him sent to Oxford around 1492. While there, More immersed himself in Greek, Latin, French, history, mathematics, and philosophy. He stayed for two years and then was compelled by his father to leave in order to study law at New Inn in London. In February 1496, he was admitted as a student to Lincoln's Inn, another London law school; once he had qualified as a lawyer, he stayed on as a popular lecturer.

Although law absorbed much of More's time (as he laments in a preface to *Utopia*), he continued to pursue his studies and in 1497 was delighted to meet the famous Dutch scholar Desiderius Erasmus, with whom he became good friends; many of their letters survive.

In 1504, More was elected to Parliament, where he defended the free speech of Members and opposed Henry VII's demand for a heavy round of taxation. The taxes were reduced, but an angry King arranged to have More's father arrested on a trumped-up charge and More himself expelled. More returned to public life only in 1509, when Henry VIII came to the throne. In 1505, he married Jane Colt; theirs was a happy marriage that produced four children before Jane's death six years later. Grieving, but wanting a mother for his children, More married Alice Middleton, a widow, a month after his first wife's death. He arranged an excellent education for all his children, including his daughters, and was particularly proud of young Margaret's scholarly accomplishments. Erasmus claimed More had once considered becoming a monk, living for a while in the London Charterhouse, a monastery for Carthusian monks. Ultimately he evidently decided against this, choosing (as More himself explained) to be "a chaste husband rather than an impure priest." But his early attraction to communal and penitential ways did not disappear; it may well underlie More's wearing of a hair shirt and *Utopia*'s stress on a communal way of life.

In succeeding years, More held several political offices. In 1515, he joined a trade embassy that spent six months in Flanders, where he used his leisure time to begin *Utopia*, which was published the following year. Upon his return to England, More joined the court of Henry VIII. He developed a warm but uneasy relationship with the King, and over the next two decades he received many honors: knighted in 1521, he was elected Speaker of the House in 1523 and appointed High Steward of Cambridge University in 1525. In 1529, More succeeded Cardinal Wolsey as Lord Chancellor, England's highest political position next to the king's. His first responsibility was to serve as Chief Justice, a position he filled with skill and honesty, introducing reforms that streamlined the judicial system. More was also responsible for enforcing anti-heresy laws (like many at the time, More believed that heresy threatened political stability as well as souls). He not only prosecuted some he called "heretics" but wrote strident denunciations of Martin Luther, William Tyndale, and others, becoming in turn a target of Protestant polemics.

More's greatest challenge was to deal with the "King's great matter," Henry's claim that his marriage to Catherine of Aragon was invalid and that he was free to marry Anne Boleyn. Pope Clement VII refused to agree to an annulment or a divorce, and Henry eventually renounced papal authority and declared himself to be head of the English Church. More could not support the King's actions, although he did not publicly reject them and indeed insisted on his right to keep his opinions private. In May 1532, he resigned.

In March 1534, Parliament passed Henry's Act of Succession. This legislation required certain of the King's ministers and subjects to take the Oath of Supremacy, which stated that the King's children by

Anne Boleyn were legitimate heirs to the throne. Those who took the Oath were also required to repudiate all foreign authority, including that of the Pope. On 14 April 1534, More was asked to swear. He refused and was sent to the Tower of London. There he wrote letters and religious works, including the serene and surprisingly funny *Dialogue of Comfort Against Tribulation*, until the authorities confiscated his writing implements. On 1 July 1535, More was indicted for high treason, found guilty, and sentenced to hang, although the King commuted the sentence to a more humane method of execution, beheading. More was executed on Tower Hill on 6 July, reportedly saying, "I die the King's good servant but God's first." His body was buried in the Church of St. Peter and his head was displayed on London Bridge for a month. On 19 May 1935, Pope Pius XI declared More a saint.

Renaissance Humanism

Thomas More is often described as exemplifying the spirit of Renaissance humanism; it is a concept worth spending some time on by way of background both to More and to *Utopia*. Nowadays the word "humanist" often is taken to imply opposition to religion in general, and to Christianity in particular. The opposite is the case with Renaissance humanism, particularly north of Italy. Humanists were distinguished from other scholars not by exclusive focus on human or secular texts, but rather by their focus on secular writings, particularly classical ones, *as well as* on religious texts and thought. Thus Erasmus produced books on Graeco-Roman culture *and* editions of the New Testament in the original Greek and of works by patristic writers. In one key particular, humanism was in accord with Protestant thought: Erasmus and many other humanists supported making the Bible available in the vernacular. But—as attested by More's willingness to die rather than approve England's separation from Roman Catholicism—humanists tended to be more willing than Luther or, later, Calvin to remain connected to Roman Catholic tradition. (Erasmus, for example, favored reform within the Catholic Church but opposed a full Protestant Reformation.)

The recovery and reappraisal of works from classical Greece and Rome was central to Renaissance humanism—as it had been to medieval scholasticism centuries earlier. The recovery of texts by the scholastics, however, had entailed stress on applying classical learning to theological ends; had placed particular emphasis on the works of Aristotle; and had displayed a strong tendency to treat classical writings as authoritative. For Renaissance humanists, classical writings were of interest for many purposes: the epic poems of Homer and Virgil and the erotic poems of Ovid were of as much interest as the writings of the philosophers. And many humanists felt little obligation to demonstrate that a seemingly new idea in fact accorded with ancient authority; Renaissance humanism was often prepared to break new ground, and to acknowledge breaking it.

Of the Greek philosophers, Plato, rather than Aristotle, came to the fore. Of particular importance was the Platonic concept of ideal forms—the notion that for every physical object, metaphysical concept, and ethical principle there is an ideal abstract form that in fact is more "real" than its manifestations in the actual or material world. It is not difficult to see how Platonic "ideas" could be harmonized with Christian ideals, and many humanist thinkers endeavored to do just that.[1] But Platonic philosophy also lent force to the sometime humanist impulse (felt particularly in Italy) to celebrate humanity itself, if not without reference to a Creator then with unprecedented emphasis on human potential and free will. A groundbreaking text here was the *Oration on the Dignity of Man* (1486) by the Florentine writer Pico della Mirandola. As Pico saw it,

> upon man, at the moment of his creation, God bestowed seeds pregnant with all possibilities, the germs of every form of life. Whichever of these a man shall cultivate, the same will mature and bear fruit in him. If vegetative, he will become a plant; if sensual, he will become brutish; if rational, he will reveal himself as a heavenly being; if intellectual, he will be an angel and the son of God... Who then will not look with awe upon this our chameleon?

The contrast between Pico's confidence in human potential and the emphasis both in medieval Christianity and in the theology of the French Protestant John Calvin (1509–64) on the inherent sinfulness of man (and even more so of woman) could hardly be more marked.

---

1   Some writers (e.g., Spenser and Rabelais) welcomed Platonism's vision of a world of ideas to which we can rise, but also stressed God's descent into the world of flesh.

Northern humanists such as Erasmus and More were less optimistic than was Pico about human nature, but in their work, too, we may see the possibility of imagining human society as a body independent of the workings of God. The supreme English example is More's *Utopia*, which imagines, although with a countering irony and ambivalence, the transformation of a culture through fundamentally different but entirely human-made social structures and practices.

More's Writing of *Utopia*: The Background

Even a brief look at the variety—and the interconnectedness—of the life More led during the period leading up to the writing of *Utopia* may offer illuminating perspectives on the work. A lawyer by training, More had attended Parliament as a representative of the London merchants. In 1510 he had been appointed to the post of under-sheriff in London (one of two such positions); his responsibility was to act on behalf of the sheriff at the Sheriff's Court, held once a week at the Guildhall. Acting in this capacity until 1518, he dealt with a wide variety of matters and had a great deal of contact with the criminal elements of society. Theft, assault, rape, and arson were among the many sorts of cases he tried; many of those convicted were sentenced to death (even petty theft could be a capital offence). According to Erasmus he developed a reputation for fairness, and was widely regarded with affection as well as respect. He must also have developed a keen sense of the issues surrounding capital punishment, and inevitably he would have developed a knowledge of the effects that poverty and disease may have on human lives. But at the same time he was becoming more and more well-connected with people of influence and power both in London and in the country as a whole. He advised various city bodies on legal matters, he acted as a spokesman and legal representative for groups as diverse as the fishmongers, the mercers, the bakers, and various groups of tradesmen, and he began frequently to play a significant negotiating role in the concluding of agreements involving these groups. He was appointed as a commissioner of sewers along the Thames; he lectured regularly on legal matters at Lincoln's Inn; he maintained his own (increasingly flourishing) legal practice; he met frequently with the archbishop of Canterbury and became intimately familiar with many Church affairs; he maintained contact with many of the leading thinkers of the day; he wrote his *History of Richard III*; he began to become involved in Court and diplomatic circles. Given the scope of his experience, it is hardly surprising that, when an English delegation was being formed in 1515 to try to resolve various commercial disputes with Flanders over the vital wool trade, both the king's council and the Merchant Adventurers asked that More be a part of the delegation.

The negotiations turned out to be far more protracted than had been expected—they dragged on intermittently for several months— but they were far from all-consuming, particularly for someone as used to a busy schedule as More was. He spent some time complaining about the lack of activity (and about the meager pay for those attached to the delegation), but he also spent a great deal of time engaged in intellectual pursuits. Aside from *Utopia*, the most notable of his 1515 writings is perhaps a long letter he wrote to the theologian Martin Dorp in defense of Erasmus, whose projects at the time included a comparison of the then-standard Latin (Vulgate) text of the New Testament with that of the original Greek with a view to identifying misleading or erroneous passages in the Vulgate. Dorp was among those conservative voices in the Church who were suspicious of such work, seeing no need for scholarly initiatives that might lead to challenges to traditional interpretations of Christian texts. But More's arguments for the value of such scholarship were effective; Dorp withdrew his criticisms, and Erasmus's work went forward.[1]

While in Flanders More stayed for several weeks in Antwerp with Peter Giles, Chief Secretary to the city and, like More, a good friend of Erasmus. Like More, too, Giles was concerned with questions of justice and fairness; with economic matters and with civic govern-

---

1   The controversy over Erasmus's project extended across Europe, and also involved broader disputes as to the relative merits of Greek and Roman traditions, with some followers of Erasmus answering those who opposed the new Greek scholarship with attacks on traditions of Roman philosophy. Some have argued that this controversy is central to the background of *Utopia*; Eric Nelson, for example, has argued that More's work dramatizes "a confrontation between the values of the Roman republican tradition and those of a rival commonwealth theory based on Greek ethics. "Utopia" suggests that, when seen from a Roman perspective, Greek advice looks like "nonsense." But, for More, that "nonsense" yields the "best state of a commonwealth." See Eric Nelson, "Greek Nonsense in More's Utopia," *The Historical Journal*, vol. 44, no. 4 (Dec. 2001), 889–917.

ance; with crime and punishment; and with international affairs. The two spent a good deal of time in conversation and became friends. It was during his time in Antwerp that More conceived of the idea of writing *De Optimo Reipublicae Statu* (as the work that came to be known as *Utopia* was originally entitled)—"The Best Condition of a Society." Eventually, More made Giles a central figure in *Utopia*, and Giles played an important role in arranging for the printing and dissemination of the work.

Utopia

More's *Utopia* has given its name to an entire genre (though many would argue that the genre of utopian fiction predates *Utopia*); "utopia" has come to signify any work describing a seemingly idyllic, fictional society. But to what extent is More's *Utopia* a utopia? This elusive and sometimes playful text resists any simple categorization or interpretation. The text can be read convincingly as moral allegory, political manifesto, or elaborate literary joke. And if *Utopia* is indeed meant to illustrate an ideal, it is a matter of much debate what that ideal is; the text has frequently been read as presenting an idealized version of (what we now refer to as) socialist or communist society, but it has also been read as presenting an idealized version of classical Greek society and as presenting an idealized version of Catholic society. Conflicting interpretations of More's life and beliefs have been brought into the debate as historians and literary critics have attempted to solve the puzzle of the work's meaning through appeals to authorial intention. But *Utopia* has stubbornly resisted efforts to fix its meaning.

In part this resistance to fixity may be attributed to the work's form. More seems to have written the second part of the work first, and some time later to have added the opening book, setting the second in context, but also problematizing any interpretation tending towards taking Book 2 at face value; the two-book structure of the final work militates against interpretations that would resolve its meaning into a neatly unified whole. In part, too, *Utopia*'s elusiveness may be attributed to complexity of narrative viewpoint; multiple layers of narrative voice allow ample space for multiple readings (for example, of the degree to which irony may be at play), and work to steer readers away from readings that exclusively privilege a single point of view.

More's *Utopia* (like other Renaissance texts with utopian themes, such as Francis Bacon's *The New Atlantis* and Henry Neville's *The Isle of Pines*), is deeply steeped in classical tradition: More's text serves as a commentary on classical meditations on the characteristics of an ideal commonwealth—most notably that of Plato in his *Republic*, *Timaeus*, and *Laws*. (More was no doubt aware as well of the views of Aristotle on such matters, as set out in his *Politics*, but the Platonic influence clearly predominates over the Aristotelian.) In Plato's *Republic* the guardians of an ideal society are obliged to ensure that property is held in common, everyone is obliged to work, and the ideal ruler is a philosopher.) Other classical texts are also relevant; the often playful spirit of *Utopia* seems indebted to Lucian's *Satirical Sketches* and Horace's *Satires*, both of which aim to combine humor and instruction. A satirical sketch by Lucian, which was translated from Greek to Latin by More and Erasmus around 1505, may have suggested the structure of *Utopia*; in the first part of the sketch a serious issue is discussed from different points of view, and in the second the character Menippus throws light on the issue by telling the tale of a journey to an imaginary land. In other formal aspects, too, *Utopia* recalls classical authors: Book 1's dialogue form is indebted to the Dialogues of Plato and of Cicero. In the degree to which it both relies upon and reappraises classical works, then, *Utopia* is very much a characteristic work of its time.

Another key influence for *Utopia* was the burgeoning genre of travel literature. During the Renaissance, as European countries competed to explore and lay claim to large parts of Asia, Africa, and the New World, the proliferation of printed material made accounts of many voyages readily available to the literate public. Tales of incredible journeys ranged from the completely fabricated to the accurately documented, and readers had to sift the truth from the fiction. *Utopia* plays with this genre of travel narrative, purporting to be an account of a voyage undertaken by real-life explorer Amerigo Vespucci. In Book 1 Raphael Hythloday is introduced as a sailor with Vespucci, who has encountered the island of Utopia on one of his trips to the New World. The language and tone of Book 2's description of Utopia are suggestive of a travel narrative, while the playful paratexts (prefaces, maps, marginalia, and even a poem in Utopian) that accompanied early editions of *Utopia* resemble the sorts of materials that often accompanied accounts of real voyages. In the context of the possibilities presented by Renaissance exploration, the discovery of such an island would have seemed almost plausible, and this plausibility is played upon throughout the text.

Deliberate gestures towards potential reality are considered one of the defining elements of utopian texts; such works tend to go to great lengths to highlight the plausibility of the lands they describe even while, paradoxically, presenting themselves as works of fiction. Utopias are generally not set in fictional lands, or in distant past or future times. (It is a common mistake to imagine that utopias are typically set in the future.) Instead, these ideal societies tend to neighbor our own; explanations are typically provided as to why they have remained hidden for so long, and how they were discovered. Further, human nature is generally shown to be as we sense it to be from our own experience—members of society are as likely to put their own needs first as they are to give preference to the collective well-being. Economic realities relating to supply and demand still apply, and the same problems of limited resources present themselves. What makes a utopia ideal, then, is not its citizens or its superior environment, but its superior social organization.

The social organization of Utopia—and the ways in which it contrasts with that of England—is the central focus of More's work. Book 1 is set up as a conversation between More, his friend Peter Giles, and Raphael Hythloday, to whom More is introduced by Giles. The three debate the social problems of England, with Raphael denouncing many aspects of the way in which society is organized, from the system of land ownership to the practice of executing thieves when the poor have often been forced by poverty to turn to theft or begging for survival. In Book 2 Raphael provides, by way of contrast, a glowing description of the island of Utopia's social structures and customs. A central principle is collective ownership; private property has been abolished in order to end poverty and curb human greed and pride. (This economic system is presented in contrast to that of England, in which supposedly holy men "enclose every bit of land for pasture, pull down houses, and destroy towns," and wealth is "divvied up among a few, who leave nothing to the rest but poverty.")

But it is not only pride and greed that have been curbed; Utopia, it seems, has also eliminated such things as religious conflict and idleness, and greatly reduced criminal activity. It is a society that allows a then-unprecedented degree of equality to women. Without a revealed religion, Utopians privilege rationality, make happiness their highest good, and permit both divorce and euthanasia.

On the face of it, Book 2 presents ways of organizing society that would largely provide solutions to the problems discussed in Book 1. But clearly the relationship between the two is less straightforward than that; no reader should presume a stable relationship between Utopian society and that of Renaissance England in which the former is to be consistently taken as superior to the latter. The reference in Book 2 to the Utopian language retaining "some traces of Greek in the names of their cities and officers" is a pointer; "Utopia" derives from the Greek for "no place." Are we to take that to suggest simply that such a place does not and never has existed on earth, or to suggest that it would not be feasible or advisable to try to emulate the practices of the utopians on earth? Similar examples abound. The name "Raphael" links the character with the Archangel Raphael (Hebrew for "God has healed"), but his last name, "Hythloday," is derived from the Greek for "speaker of nonsense." Utopia's main river, "Anyder," means "waterless" in Greek, while "Polylerites" means "land of much nonsense." Nor are the facts provided about life in Utopia entirely straightforward. We are told that Utopians never resort to the death penalty—but later learn that if prisoners break any of the rules when they are in bonded labor, the penalty is death. Utopian society is lauded for the liberties it gives its citizens, but the Utopians seem in practice to have little freedom or leisure time, and are expected to spend their non-working hours in service to the community. Throughout Book 2 the character of "More," while recounting Raphael's tale, periodically interrupts the narrative with comments that throw into question the reliability of the account; he misses some of what Raphael says, and is unsure as to certain details. More broadly, the very structure of dialogue-within-dialogue keeps us as readers at a distance, with the layers of narrative acting almost as filters.

The elusiveness of the characters casts further doubt on who and what we are meant to believe. The text seems to set up "More" and

Raphael as opposites, yet many of the biographical details of Raphael's life correspond exactly to those of the real More (both served as pages in the household of Cardinal Morton, and both had doubts about the advisability of a career as counselor to a prince). But any attempt to see Raphael as embodying aspects or beliefs of More the author is surely problematic, given that many Utopian practices Raphael praises would have been opposed by More (a devout Catholic who died for his faith)—for example, divorce and remarriage, euthanasia, and expressions of pagan beliefs.

It is impossible fully to divine More's intentions in writing *Utopia*, but the text makes it equally impossible to avoid raising the question of authorial intent. It is hard to say which aspects of Utopian society More most admired, but it is impossible to avoid interpreting much of the work as legitimate criticism of European folly. It is hard to say which specifics of Utopian life may be intended to be seen as exemplary, but difficult not to feel that the author approves of an overarching spirit of self-sacrifice for the good of a community. Beyond that, however, generalizations are hazardous. And perhaps More's text is meant to serve only as a challenge to the reader's assumptions; More's imaginary world surely prompts readers see themselves and their society in a new light—a goal shared by nearly all writers of utopian fiction since.

What of *Utopia*'s recurring discussions of the appropriate role of private property in society? The character "More" asserts that "life can never be happy or satisfying where all things are held in common," but, as author, More seems to give Raphael stronger arguments than he does "More." It is almost impossible to read the argument of "More" in the book's final paragraph as having been intended without irony; the suggestion by "More" that the principle of living communally and sharing goods should be rejected out of hand because enacting it would have a deleterious effect on "splendor and majesty" must surely be satire. Much as the abolition of private property may to modern readers suggest Communist principles, we should not forget that such notions are also in accord with the principles of the early Christian Church: Acts 4:32 says of the followers of Jesus that none of them said that any of the things "which he possessed was his own, but that they had all things common." Yet equally, there is a good deal of what we know of More's life that has led scholars to doubt that the author of *Utopia* would ever in fact have advocated abolishing private property—and there are several passages in his other writings that many have argued confirm he desired no such thing.[1]

Are we in the end to take at face value the concluding thought of "More" that "there are many features of the Utopian commonwealth that I can more easily wish for in our own societies than hope to see realized"? And if so, what are those features? In the final analysis it may be that all we can with confidence conclude that "More" shares with More is the hope expressed as the group is called to dinner that "there would be time to think more deeply about these matters and to discuss them more fully." *Utopia* provides an extraordinary wealth of material for thought and discussion, but we shall never be quite sure what parts of it the author intended us to take seriously. In this the work is very much in accord with what we know of its author; though Thomas More was clearly a man of great gravitas and high principle, he was also, according to his great grandson, a man who "spoke always so sadly that few could see by his looke whether he spoke in earnest or in jeaste."[2]

---

1   The passage that has been taken by many commentators as perhaps most clearly indicating a rejection of a communal approach to wealth and property appears in More's 1535 English work *A Dialogue of Comfort against Tribulation* and is included in the appendices to this edition. Even if we accept that passage as having such an implication, however, we should remember that this work was written almost 20 years after *Utopia*; like many people, More may have been a good deal less egalitarian in his political beliefs in his mid fifties than he was in his mid thirties. For a helpful discussion of this and other such passages (and a rebuttal of various arguments suggesting that they may be taken as conclusive evidence that More was no opponent of private property) see Paul Turner, *Utopia* (London: Penguin, 2/e 2003) 114–17.

2   Cresacre More, *The Life and Death of Sir Thomas More* (1631), 235; as quoted by Peter Ackroyd, *The Life of Thomas More* (New York: Doubleday, 1998), 177.

A Note on the Text

Like the vast majority of works at the time that were written for an educated, international audience, *Utopia* is written in Latin, not English; Latin served as a "universal" language, spoken as well as written by those with education across Europe and in some cases beyond. It was first translated into English by Ralph Robinson in 1551, and that translation continued to be widely read until well into the twentieth century.

The present text has been prepared for *The Broadview Anthology of British Literature* (and for this volume) by William P. Weaver. It is an extensive revision and modernization of the early twentieth-century translation of G.C. Richards. The Richards is generally very faithful to the Latin, both in diction and in retaining to a high degree the syntax of More's Latin. But it is in some respects inaccurate, and it does not read at all smoothly in English—particularly for readers in the twenty-first century. The present revision endeavors to strike a balance between fidelity to the original Latin and readability for a modern English-speaking audience. Latinate sentence structures have been simplified. Many of the original parallelisms have been retained but tightened up to some degree. The translation strives to convey the rhetorical feel of More's argumentative style—especially its frequent litotes and irony—while keeping sentences to a manageable length for the modern reader. At the same time, the sentence structures have not been fully regularized; it would be impossible to do so without losing much of the colloquial style in which More writes (or Raphael speaks) *Utopia*.

In its diction, too, the present translation tries to convey more of More's colloquialism than one finds in a translation such as the Richards, while not losing More's sense of formality—and to convey the plain meaning of the original in the common currency of today's English. "Make a hotchpotch of tragedy and comedy" becomes "mangle a perfectly good comedy," and "one insatiable glutton" becomes "one fat cat."

Modern translations differ widely in the degree to which they take liberties with the original in the interests of making the text relevant politically to the modern reader. An interesting point of comparison, for example, is the Latin "ubi omnia sint communia." The phrase is given a fairly close literal translation in these pages—

> "I can't agree," I said. "Life can never be happy or satisfying **where all things are held in common.**"

Similarly, the translation of the distinguished More scholar George Logan has

> "But I don't see it that way," I replied. "It seems to me that people cannot possibly live well **when all things are held in common.**"

The popular Paul Turner translation, in contrast, uses phrasing that suggests a stronger connection to the nineteenth-century ideas of Karl Marx than it does to Platonic or Christian notions:

> "I disagree. I don't believe you'd ever have a reasonable standard of living **under a communist system.**"

There can be no doubt that parallels between ideas found in *Utopia* and those of modern socialists and Marxists make for fruitful discussion—and an argument may be made that embedding such parallels in the text makes for a livelier read today. The present editors have felt it preferable, however, not to embed such parallels in the translation.

A notable feature of early editions of *Utopia* is the inclusion of numerous annotations in the margins. These marginal glosses are generally believed to have been added by Peter Giles and/or by Erasmus. Often interesting in themselves, they also provide a real sense of the way in which the intellectual community of the time operated in a collaborative fashion. This edition includes all the significant glosses, albeit in the form of footnotes rather than marginal notations; each such note begins with the heading [marginal note] in square brackets.

Utopia

Concerning the Best State of
a Commonwealth and
the New Island of Utopia

A Truly Golden Handbook,
No Less Beneficial than Entertaining,
By the Distinguished and Eloquent Author.

THOMAS MORE
Citizen and Sheriff[1] of the Famous City of London

---

1   *Sheriff* More had been appointed Undersheriff of London in 1510. The position sometimes entailed acting in the capacity of a judge as well as representing the Sheriff.

THOMAS MORE TO PETER GILES[1]

I am almost ashamed, my dear Peter Giles, to send you this little book about the Utopian commonwealth after nearly a year, for I am sure you expected it within a month and a half. Certainly you know that I was relieved of all the labor of gathering materials for it and had to give no thought to their arrangement. I had only to repeat what in your company I had heard Raphael relate. There was no reason for me to take trouble over the style of the narrative; first, his language was hurried and impromptu, and then, to make matters worse, spoken by one who was, as you know, less acquainted with Latin than with Greek. Therefore the nearer my style resembles his careless simplicity the closer it comes to the truth, which here is my main concern.

I confess my dear Peter, that all these considerations relieved me of so much trouble that scarcely anything remained for me to do. Otherwise gathering and arranging materials would have required much time and attention from someone with wits neither the slightest nor the most ignorant. Had the task required writing down the material not only accurately but eloquently, I could not have performed it, no matter how much time and effort I might expend. But, as it was, since those burdensome cares had been removed and it remained only to write out simply what I had heard, I had no difficulty at all. And yet my other obligations left me practically no leisure to finish this trifling task. I am constantly engaged in legal business, either pleading or hearing, either giving an award as arbiter or deciding a case as judge. I pay a courtesy visit to one person and go on business to another. I devote almost the whole day to other people's affairs and what little is left to my own. For myself, that is for learning, I leave nothing at all. When I have return home I must talk with my wife, chat with my children, and confer with my servants. All this activity I count as business if it must be done—and it must be done, unless you want to be a stranger in your own home. Besides, one must take care to be as agreeable as possible to those whom nature has supplied,

---

1 *Peter Giles* Giles (c. 1486–1533), a friend of More's, was a scholar who also worked for the city of Antwerp. As has been noted by scholars of More, in this letter and in *Utopia* More plays with words meaning "all," "nothing," and "nowhere" often exploiting, in the letter to Giles, the rhetorical figure "litotes" (denying the contrary, as in "not nowhere" to mean "somewhere"). Even at the lexical level, then, More's text is a not unsmiling venture into paradox of the sort Renaissance humanists found not unappealing.

chance has made, or you yourself have chosen to be the companions of your life, provided you do not spoil them by kindness or through indulgence make masters of your servants.

Amid such occupations, the day, the month, and the year slip away. When, then, can I find time to write? Nor have I said a word about sleep, nor even about food, which for many people takes up as much time as sleep—and sleep takes up almost half a man's life. So I have for myself only the time I filch from sleep and food. Slowly, therefore, because this time is so little, and yet at last, because this time is something, I have finished *Utopia* and sent it to you, my dear Peter, to read—and to remind me of anything that has escaped me.

In this respect I do not entirely distrust myself, wishing only that I were as nimble in intelligence and learning as I am not altogether deficient in memory. Nevertheless, I am not so confident as to believe that I have forgotten nothing. As you know, John Clement,[1] my pupil-servant, was also present at the conversation. Indeed I do not allow him to absent himself from any profitable talk, for from this young plant, which has begun to put forth green shoots in Greek and Latin literature, I expect no small harvest someday. He has made very doubtful concerning one point: according to my own recollection, Hythlodaeus[2] declared that the bridge spanning the river Anydrus[3] at Amaurotum[4] is five hundred paces in length. But my John says that two hundred must be subtracted, for the river there is not more than three hundred paces in breadth. Please recall the matter to mind. If you agree with him, I shall adopt the same view and think myself mistaken. If you do not remember, I shall put down, as I have actually done, what I myself seem to remember. Just as I shall take great pains to have nothing incorrect in the book, so, if there is doubt about anything, I would rather tell an objective falsehood than an intentional lie—for I would rather be honest than clever.

It would be easy for you to remedy this defect if you were to ask Raphael himself, either in person or by letter. You must do so because of another doubt that has arisen, whether through my fault

---

1 *John Clement* Clement (d. 1572), later a leading scholar and physician to Henry VIII, was at this time tutor to More's children.
2 *Hythlodaeus* Greek: knowledgeable about nonsense.
3 *Anydrus* Greek: without water.
4 *Amaurotum* Greek: made dim.

or through yours or through Raphael's I do not know. We forgot to ask, and he forgot to say, where in the New World Utopia is located. I am sorry that point got omitted, and I would be willing to pay a considerable sum to purchase the information, partly because I am somewhat embarrassed not to know in what sea lies the very island of which I am saying so much, and partly because there are several among us (and one in particular, a devout man and a theologian by profession) burning with an extraordinary desire to visit Utopia. The theologian wishes to go not from an idle taste for sight-seeing in novel places, but in order to foster and promote our religion, begun there so felicitously. To carry out this plan properly, he has decided to ask the Pope to send him there and, what is more, to name him Bishop of Utopia. He has no scruple in pressing for this appointment, since he considers it a holy suit, motivated not by desire for honor or gain but by piety.

Therefore I beg you, my dear Peter, either in person, if you conveniently can, or by letter if he has gone, to reach Hythlodaeus and make sure that my work includes nothing false and omits nothing true. I am inclined to think that it would be better to show him the book itself. No one else is so well able to correct any mistake, and he cannot do me this favor unless he reads through what I have written. In this way, moreover, you will determine whether he accepts with pleasure or suffers with annoyance my composition of this work. If he has decided to write about his adventures himself, perhaps he might not want me to do so. In making known the commonwealth of Utopia, I certainly do not wish to forestall him or to rob his own narrative of novelty's flower and charm. Nevertheless, to tell the truth, I have not yet made up my own mind whether or not to publish this. So varied are the tastes of mortals, so peevish the characters of some, so ungrateful their dispositions and wrongheaded their judgments, that those who blithely indulge their desires seem better off than those who torment themselves with anxiety in order to publish something meant to bring profit or pleasure to those who all too often receive it with disdain or ingratitude.

Many are ignorant of learning; many despise it. The barbarian rejects as harsh whatever is not utterly barbarian. Those with pretensions to learning despise as trite whatever is not packed with obsolete expressions. Some approve only of what is old; many admire only their own work. This fellow is so grim he will not hear of a joke; that fellow is too insipid to endure wit. Some are so dull-minded that they fear all satire as much as someone bitten by a rabid dog fears water. Others are so fickle that when sitting they praise one thing and when standing praise another. Some lounge in taverns and over their cups criticize the talents of authors. With much pontificating and self-indulgence, they condemn each one for his writings, plucking each one, as it were, by the hair. They themselves remain under cover and, as the saying goes, out of range. They are so smooth and shaven that they present not even one honest hair by which they might be caught. Others are so ungrateful that although delighted with the work they do not love the author any the better. They are not unlike discourteous guests who, after being freely entertained at a rich banquet, go home well filled but without thanking the host who invited them. So go ahead and spread a feast at your own expense for men of such dainty palates, of such varied tastes, and of such unforgetful and grateful natures!

At any rate, my dear Peter, consult with Hythlodaeus on the matter I mentioned. Later I shall be fully free to reopen that case for new debate. Now that I have gone through the labor of writing, however, it is too late for me to be wise. Therefore, provided it be done with the consent of Hythlodaeus, in the matter of publishing in everything that remains I shall follow the advice of my friends—and above all yours. Good-bye, my sweetest friend, and my regards to your excellent wife. Love me as you have ever done, for I love you more than ever.

Utopia
The Best State of a Commonwealth, The Discourse of the Extraordinary Character, Raphael Hythlodaeus, as Reported by the Renowned Figure, Thomas More, Citizen and Sheriff of the Famous City of Great Britain, London.

Book 1

The most invincible King of England, Henry VIII, a prince adorned with incomparable virtues, recently found himself involved in a dispute, over matters of no little weight, with His Serene Highness Charles, King of Castile.[1] To discuss these things and negotiate a settlement he sent me on an embassy to Flanders, along with the peerless Cuthbert Tunstall, whom recently, to the great satisfaction of all,[2] he has named Master of the Rolls.[3] Of his praises I shall say nothing, not because I fear that the testimony of a friend might be disbelieved, but because his merit and his learning are too much for me to describe and too well known for me to attempt the task, lest I should display the brightness of the sun with a candle, as the proverb has it.[4]

---

1   *Charles ... Castile*   Charles V (1500–58), Holy Roman Emperor (1519–58), was also King of Spain (1516–56), but at the time referred to here had not yet risen to such heights. The "weighty matters" were commercial matters concerning the prohibition of wool sales to the Netherlands.

2   [marginal note]   Cuthbert Tunstall. [More published *Utopia* through his friend Peter Giles, a humanist scholar city official in Antwerp; Erasmus was also consulted. Early editions of the work include numerous marginal glosses, which, it has been widely speculated, were additions by Giles and/or Erasmus. The more significant of these glosses are included in the present volume in the footnotes rather than in the margin.]

3   *Cuthbert Tunstall*   Prominent member of the clergy (1474–1559) who was appointed Archdeacon of Chester at the time of this diplomatic mission; *Master of the Rolls* Principal Clerk of the Chancery Court (a court of appeals).

4   [marginal note]   Adage.

We were greeted at Bruges, the place appointed for our meeting, by the king of Castile's commissioners, all notable men, at the head of whom was the great Margrave of Bruges.[1] But the chief speaker, and the ablest of them all, was George de Theimsecke, Provost of Cassel,[2] a man not only trained in eloquence but a natural orator, highly learned in the law, moreover, and a clever diplomat of much experience. When after several meetings there were certain points on which we could not agree, they bade us farewell for a few days and left for Brussels to learn their king's will. Meanwhile I myself, as my business led me, made my way to Antwerp.

While I stayed there I had various visitors. Most welcome of all[3] was Peter Giles, a native of Antwerp, where he is highly esteemed and respectably employed (somewhat beneath his merit), a young man both learned and prudent. He is most virtuous, cultured, and courteous, and to his friends so open-hearted, affectionate, loyal and sincere, that you will scarcely find his match in all the annals of friendship. He is unusually modest, exceptionally honest, and second to none for plain good sense. In conversation he is so polished and so witty (without ever giving offence) that though I missed hearth and home, wife and children terribly (for it had been more than four months since I left), his delightful society and charming discourse relieved me of my homesickness.

One day I had been at divine service in Notre Dame, the finest church in the city and the most crowded with worshippers. Mass being over, I was about to return to my lodging when I happened to see Peter conversing with a stranger, a man of advanced years with sunburnt countenance and long beard, his cloak hanging carelessly from his shoulder; his appearance and dress looked to me like those of a seafarer. When Peter saw me, he came up to greet me, but before I could return his salutation he drew me a little aside and said, pointing to the one with whom I had seen him talking, "Do you see this man? I was on the point of taking him straight to you."

"He would have been very welcome," said I, "for your sake."

"No," said he, "if you knew him, then for his own sake. There is no man alive today who can give you such an account of unknown peoples and lands. I know you're passionate to hear such tales."

---

1 *Bruges* Significant port for the wool trade.
2 *Provost of Cassel* I.e., Chief Magistrate of Cassel.
3 [marginal note] Peter Giles.

"Well, then," said I, "my guess was not a bad one. The moment I saw him, I was sure he was a ship's captain."

"But you are quite mistaken," said he, "for his sailing has not been like that of Palinurus but of Ulysses, or rather like that of Plato.[1] Now this Raphael, for that was his name (Hythlodaeus was his family name), was something of a Latinist, but an expert in Greek. He was less studious of the Roman tongue because he was entirely devoted to philosophy and knew that Latin had little to offer him there, except for a few things by Seneca and Cicero.[2] Eager to see the world, he left his worldly goods at home with his brothers (he is Portuguese) and joined Amerigo Vespucci.[3] He was his constant companion on the last three of those four voyages about which everyone has read. In the end, he did not accompany him home, for he pestered, even harassed Amerigo to let him be one of the twenty-four left behind at the fort during the last voyage. And so, to let him have his way, they left him behind, more anxious for travel than over the place of his death; for these two sayings are constantly on his lips: 'He who has no grave is covered by the sky,' and, 'From all places it is the same distance to heaven.'[4] But for the grace of God, this determination of his would have cost him dear. In any case, after Amerigo had set sail, Raphael traveled with five companions from the fort through many countries and came by sheer luck to Ceylon, and thence to Calcutta,[5] where by good fortune he found some Portuguese ships. And so, after much time and beyond all exectation, he returned home."

After Peter finished his story, I thanked him for his kindness in going to such lengths to introduce me to one whose conversation he hoped would give me pleasure; then I turned to Raphael. We greeted each other, exchanging the civilities that commonly pass at the first

---

1 *Palinurus* Aeneas's steersman, who falls asleep at the helm and is tossed overboard in the *Aeneid*; *Ulysses* His story is told variously in the *Iliad*, the *Odyssey* and the *Aeneid*; *Plato* Greek philosopher (c. 427–347 BCE).

2 *Seneca* Roman philosopher, playwright and orator (c. 4 BCE–65 CE); *Cicero* Roman statesman, philosopher, and orator, who was stoical in many of his attitudes (c. 106–43 BCE).

3 *Amerigo Vespucci* Noted Italian explorer (1451–1512), Vespucci was one of the explorers of the "New World," for whom it is named America.

4 [marginal note] Aphorism. [These are paraphrases of Lucan's *Pharsalia*, 8.819, and Cicero's *Tusculan Disputations* 1.43.104, respectively.]

5 *Ceylon* Island (now the nation of Sri Lanka) located in the Indian Ocean off the coast of India; *Calcutta* Port city on the eastern coast of India.

meeting of strangers, and then went off to my house,where we sat down to talk in the garden, on a bench covered with turves of grass.

Raphael told us how, after the departure of Vespucci, he and the friends who had stayed behind in the fort slowly ingratiated themselves with the natives. Little by little, after continued meetings and civilities, they were not only welcome but even treated as familiars. They were, moreover, in favor and good repute with a chief (whose name and country I have forgotten). He said that the chief, out of generosity, provided him and his five companions with ample provisions and travel money, as well as with a trusty guide for their journey (which was partly by water and partly in carriages over land) who could take them to other princes bearing careful recommendations in their favor.

After traveling many days, he said, they found towns and cities and very populous commonwealths with excellent institutions. To be sure, under the Equator, and on both sides of it as far as the sun's orbit extends, there lie waste deserts, scorched with continual heat. This offers an altogether sad and desolate sight, rough and uncultivated, inhabited by wild animals, snakes, and men as savage and dangerous as animals. But when you have gone a little farther, gradually the country assumes a milder aspect, the climate is less fierce, the ground covered with a pleasant green herbage, and the living creatures less wild. At length you reach peoples, cities and towns that maintain a continual traffic by sea and land, not only with each other and their neighbors but also with far-off countries. This gave him the chance to visit many countries in all directions, for there was not a ship trimmed to sail, no matter where, that did not welcome him and his companions. The ships they saw first were flat-bottomed, with the sails made of sheets of papyrus, and sometimes of leather, stitched together on willow branches. Afterwards they found ships with pointed keels and canvas sails, in all respects like ours. The mariners were skilled in dealing with the sea and weather, although he won their favor by showing them how to use a compass. Because they had not known about such an instrument before, they had hesitated to trust themselves to the sea, doing so only in the summer; but now, trusting the compass, they no longer fear stormy weather and have become dangerously confident. So this instrument, expected to be of great use, may turn out to be one of great mischief because of their lack of prudence.

It would be a long tale to report what Raphael said he saw in each place, and that is not the purpose of this book. Perhaps on another occasion I shall tell his story, especially concerning those good and wise institutions that he noticed in civilized nations. We asked him eagerly about such things, and he was more than willing to converse at length, leaving out, however, the sort of marvelous reports that are really old news. For Scyllas and greedy Harpies and cannibal Laestrygonians[1] are common enough, but well and wisely trained citizens are not to be found everywhere. Just as he noted many ill-advised customs among these strange nations, however, so too he mentioned not a few matters from which our own cities, nations, races, and kingdoms could use as models in correcting our own errors. These, as I said, I must save for another occasion. For now, I will merely relate what he told us of the manners and customs of the Utopians, first, however, recounting the conversation that led him to mention that commonwealth.

Raphael touched with wisdom on the faults of this part of the world and of that, finding many in both, and compared the wiser measures that have been taken by us and by them; for he remembered the manners and customs of each nation he visited as well as if he had lived there all his life. Peter expressed his surprise as follows: "Why, Master Raphael, I wonder that you do not attach yourself to the court of some king. I am sure there is none of them to whom you would not be very welcome, for you are capable not only of entertaining a ruler with this learning and experience of countries and people, but also of furnishing him with examples and assisting him with counsel. Thus you would not only help advance your own interests but also those of your relatives and friends."

"As for my relatives and friends," Raphael said, "I'm not much troubled about them; for I think I have pretty well performed my duty to them already. Whereas other men don't usually give up their possessions unless they are sick and old, and even then do so unwillingly, I divided my wealth among my relatives and friends when I was not just hale and hearty but young. I think they ought to be satisfied with such generosity and not ask or expect that for their sakes I would become the slave of kings."

---

1 *Scyllas ... Harpies ... Laestrygonians* Monsters of classical myth.

"Well said, my good sir!" Peter replied. " But I meant not that you should be in *servitude*, only in *service* to kings."

"One word is but a syllable shorter than the other,"[1] said Raphael.

"Whatever name you call it," said Peter, "I think it is just the right way not only to improve things for individuals and the commonwealth alike, but also to make your own condition more prosperous."

"Would I really be better off," asked Raphael, "with a way of life I completely detest? Right now I live as I please, which is more than could be said for those courtiers of yours. Besides, there are plenty of those who court the friendship of the great; and so you need not think it any great loss if they have to do without me or a few others like me."

"Well," said I, "it is plain, Master Raphael, that you desire neither riches nor power. Assuredly, I admire and look up to a man of your mind, just as much as I do to any of the high and mighty. But, I think, you will do what is worthy of you and of this generous and truly philosophic spirit of yours, if you order your life so as to apply your talent and industry to the public interest, even if so doing involves some disadvantage to yourself. This you could never do more profitably than if you were counselor to some great prince and make him follow, as I am sure you would, a straightforward and honorable course. For from the prince, as from a never failing spring, flows a stream of all that is good or evil over the whole nation. But you have such learning that even without experience of affairs you would make an excellent member of any king's council as well as such experience that even if you had no learning the same would be true."

"You are twice mistaken," said Raphael, "first in me, and then in the matter in question. For I have no such ability as you ascribe to me, and even if I did, and surrendered my leisure to affairs of state, I would not promote the public interest. For in the first place, almost all princes prefer to occupy themselves in the pursuits of war (with which I have no acquaintance nor desire any) rather than in the honorable activities of peace, and they care much more for how, by hook or by crook, they may win fresh kingdoms than how to administer well those they already have."

---

1 *One ... other* In the original Latin, the words for "in servitude to" and "in service to" are "servias" and "inservias."

"In the second place," Raphael continued, "a king's courtiers are so wise that they do not need a second opinion, or so confident that they do not want one—unless, of course, it be the opinion of one of the king's favorites. In that case, one and all eagerly approve and applaud even the stupidest of opinions, for they are studious to gain his favor by such approval. Granted, it is only natural for everyone to like his own brainchild best: the crow is delighted with his chick, the ape pleased with his cub. But if in the company of such self-seeking, such jealous men, someone should propose something that he has read was done in former times or that he has seen done in other places, they try to find fault with it, believing their whole reputation for wisdom endangered if they do not. If all else fails, they take refuge in this as a last resort: 'These things,' they say, 'were good enough for our ancestors, and we wish only we were as wise as they were.' With this argument, which they regard as unanswerable and a conclusion of the whole matter, they resume their seats, as if it were dangerous for anyone to be wiser than his forebears. It is curious—we seem to be completely oblivious of the sound opinions of our ancestors until somebody suggests something better. Then, oh, how zealously, how religiously we adhere to them! Such proud, ridiculous and obstinate prejudices I have encountered in many places, and once even in England."

"What?" I asked. "You were in our country?"

"Yes," Raphael said, "I once spent several months there, not long after the disastrous end of the Cornish revolt against the King put down with such horrible bloodshed.[1] During that time I was much indebted to the Right Reverend Father, Cardinal John Morton, Archbishop of Canterbury, at that point also Lord Chancellor[2] of England. Here was a man, Master Peter, (for Master More knows about him and needs no information from me) who deserved no less respect for his wisdom and virtue than for his authority. He was of middle stature and showed no sign of his advanced age; his countenance inspired

---

1 *disastrous … bloodshed* In 1497, in response to harsh tax burdens imposed by Henry VII, about 15,000 Cornishmen (men from Cornwall) marched on London and were brutally defeated at Blackheath.
2 *Cardinal John Morton* Cardinal, Archbishop of Canterbury, and Lord Chancellor, Morton (1420–1500) was an early patron of More and a lifelong friend; *Archbishop of Canterbury* Highest church official in England; *Lord Chancellor* High-ranking official in the House of Lords, the Lord Chancellor is the Keeper of the Great Seal of England and chief administrator of the judicial system.

respect rather than fear; his conversation was agreeable, although serious and dignified. He sometimes liked to speak sharply to petitioners, although not rudely, so as to bring out their spirit and presence of mind. Provided these capacities did not become impudence, they gave him pleasure, for he shared them and thought that they well suit those holding public office. His speech was polished and to the point and his knowledge profound; he was very able, and his memory amazingly retentive, while by learning and practice he improved his natural qualities. The King placed much confidence in his advice, and when I was there, the state seemed to depend upon him. In early youth he had been taken straight from school to court, and there he had spent his whole life in important public affairs. He suffered many turns of fortune, so that through many and great dangers he had acquired that level-headedness which, once learned, is not easily forgotten.

"One day I was at his table,"[1] continued Raphael, "when a layman, who happened to be there and was learned in the laws of your country, took some occasion to launch into a precise encomium of the severe punishments that were then meted out to thieves.[2] They were executed everywhere, he said, with as many as twenty being hanged on one gallows at a time. With so few escaping execution, he wondered by what bad luck they still so infested the country. Being free to speak my mind in front of the Cardinal, I said, 'You need not wonder; for this manner of punishing thieves goes beyond justice and is not in the public interest. It is both too harsh a penalty for theft and an insufficient deterrent. For theft is not so hideous a crime that it should cost someone his life, and no punishment, however great, will deter that man from stealing, who has no other means of getting food. In this practice, you and the greater part of the world resemble bad schoolmasters, who would rather beat than teach their scholars. You ordain grievous and terrible punishments for theft, when it would be much better to provide some means of employment; then no one would be under this terrible necessity of first stealing and then dying for it.'[3]

---

1 *One day ... his table* The dialogue over the course of the following pages is sometimes difficult to follow. Raphael recounts a long dinner-table conversation with the Cardinal, with a "layman learned in the laws" of England, with a friar, and briefly with various others. The long digression ends with Raphael's apology for telling such a lengthy tale.

2 [marginal note] Of unjust laws.

3 [marginal note] How to reduce the number of thieves.

"'We have,' the layman said, 'made sufficient provision for this. There are handicrafts and there is agriculture; they might maintain themselves by these, if they did not prefer to be rascals.'

"'No,' I said. 'You don't get away so easily. Let's say nothing of those who often come home maimed from foreign or civil wars, such as the recent fight with the Cornishmen and before that with France.[1] They have lost limbs for country and king, and now their infirmity prevents them from exercising their old crafts even while their age prevents them from learning a new one. These, I say, we can ignore, for wars come intermittently; but let us consider what happens every day. Now there are a great many idle noblemen who not only live like drones off the labors of others, such as their tenants, whom they squeeze to the utmost by raising their rents (for that is the ony way to get money they know, being otherwise so extravagant as to beggar themselves), but also carry about with them a huge crowd of parasites who have never learnt a trade by which to live. When their master dies, or they themselves fall ill, they are soon turned out, for it is easier to maintain the idle than the sick, and in any case the heir can't always support as big a household as had his father. So in the meantime their energies turn to starving, if not to thieving. For what can they do? When by a vagabond life they have worn out both clothes and health, sickly and ragged as they are, gentlemen will not engage them and country folk dare not, knowing well that someone softly brought up in idleness and luxury and has been wont to strut around in sword and buckler,[2] looking down with a swaggering expression on the whole neighborhood, and thinking himself miles above everyone, is not fit to render honest service to a poor man with spade and hoe, for scanty wage, and on frugal fare.'

"'But these,' the layman replied, 'are just the men we ought to encourage and make much of; on them, who have spirits loftier and more manly those of artisans and husbandmen, depend the strength and sinews of our army when we have to wage war.'

"'Indeed,' I said, 'you might as well say that for the sake of war we should encourage thieves. For as long as you have these men, you will never be without thieves. Just as robbers are not bad soldiers, so sol-

---

1   *not long ago ... France*   A reference to the battle at Dixmude (1489) and that at Boulogne (1492).
2   *buckler*   Small shield, usually round, that can be carried or buckled to the arm.

diers are not the most cowardly of robbers—so well do these two lines of argument agree. But this defect, though frequent with you, is not yours alone, being common to almost all nations. France in particular is sick with another more grievous plague. Even in peace (if you can call it peace) the whole country is crowded and beset with mercenaries, for the French, like you, think it smart to keep these idle retainers. These wiseacres think the public safety means having a standing army, strong and reliable, and made up chiefly of veterans, for they have no confidence in untrained men.[1] So they must always be finding an excuse for war, lest they have men without experience. They must also make sure that they are not unskilled at cutting throats, lest, as Sallust says wittily, "the hand or mind through lack of practice[2] get dull." Yet France has learned how dangerous it is to rear such wild beasts, and the examples of Rome, Carthage, Syria, and other nations show the same: not only their empires, but also their land and even their cities have been more than once destroyed by their own standing armies. How unnecessary it is to maintain them is clearly proved by this: not even the French soldiers, trained in arms from infancy, can boast that they have very often bested your fresh recruits.[3] I shall say no more, for fear of seeming to flatter you to your faces.

"'At any rate,' I went on, 'neither your town workers nor your rough and untrained farm laborers are supposed to fear the idle followers of gentlemen, unless perhaps their bodies are unfitted for strength and bravery, or whose spirits are broken by poverty. So there is no danger that those, whose bodies, once strong and vigorous (for it is only such men whom gentlemen deign to corrupt), would become weakened by idleness or enfeebled by womanly occupations if they were trained to earn their living by honest pursuits and exercised some manly toil. But, however this may be, it seems to me by in no way helpful to the commonweal to keep for the emergency of a war such a multitude of those who trouble and disturb the peace. You never have war unless you choose it, and you ought to think far more of peace. But this is not the only thing that makes thieving necessary; there is another, one I believe peculiar to you Englishmen alone.'

---

1   [marginal note]   The mischief of standing armies.
2   *Sallust*   Roman politician and historian (86–34 BCE); *hand or ... practice* Cf. Sallust's *Cataline Conspiracy*.
3   *not even ... recruits*   The English had won several decisive victories over the French.

"'What is that?' said the Cardinal.

"'Your sheep,' I replied, 'which used to be so mild and content, are now, it is said, so greedy and wild that they devour men, laying waste and depopulating fields, houses, and towns.[1] For in those parts of the realm that produce the finest and therefore most costly wool, nobles and gentlemen, and even holy abbots, are unsatisfied with the revenues and annual profits they derive from their estates.[2] No longer content with merely leading an idle life and contributing nothing good to their country, they must also do it real harm. They leave no ground to be tilled, enclose every bit of land for pasture, pull down houses, and destroy towns, leaving only a church for a barn. And, as if not enough English land were already wasted on deer parks and game preserves, these holy men turn all human habitations and cultivated land into a wilderness. Thus so that one fat cat, an insatiable and terrible scourge to his homeland, might enclose some thousand acres of tillable land in a single fence, many tenants are ejected. Some, through fraud or violence, lose their goods. Others are so wearied by oppression that they are driven to sell. Thus by hook or by crook poor wretches are compelled to leave their homes—men, women, husbands, wives, orphans, widows, parents with little children and a family not rich but numerous (for farm work requires many hands). Away they must go, I say, from hearth and home, and find no shelter. All their household furniture, which would not fetch a great price even if they could wait for a purchaser, must be sold for a trifling profit. Then as soon as they've gone through their last penny (near the beginning of their migration), what's left but to steal and hang—with justice, mind you—or wander and beg? But even wandering might land you in prison these days, for it is an "idle loitering." Nobody wants to hire their services, which they desperately offer. Why? They're accustomed to farming, and there's no need for a plow where nothing's to be sowed. It used to take several workers to cultivate a field until it was ripe for the harvest; the same field now requires only a single shepherd or rancher.

---

1 *Your sheep ... and towns* Reference to the practice of enclosure, starting in the thirteenth century, in which wealthy landlords would fence off lands previously set aside for common use, using them instead for raising sheep. This practice dislocated rural laborers and sent some into beggary, vagabondage, and even thieving.
2 *even holy abbots ... estates* The Church frequently enclosed land for its own use.

"'And so it is because of this,' I continued, 'that the price of food has risen in many parts. Wool too has gone up in price. So much so that the poor, who used to make cloth in England, cannot now afford to buy it, and so are driven from work to idleness. For after the great increase in pastureland a plague killed off a vast number of sheep. Perhaps God, vexed by the owners' display of greed, sent a murrain.[1] It might have fallen more justly on their own heads. In any case, even if the number of sheep had risen, the price wouldn't have fallen, because of the monopoly—excuse me, the *oligopoly*,[2] for there are more than one of them. Wealth stays in the hands of the same few, who are not obliged to sell before they wish, and they do not wish to sell until they get the price they ask. All other kinds of livestock are also high-priced for the same reasons, and all the more so, because as the farmhouses have been pulled down and the tillage is lessened, there are none left to raise livestock. These rich men will not rear calves as they do lambs, but buy them lean and cheap elsewhere and then, having fattened them up in their own pastures, resell them again at a tidy profit. I fear that the full mischief of this system has not yet been felt. Thus far it has raised the prices only where the animals are sold; over time, though, if the buyers remove them faster than they can be bred, then as the supply gradually diminishes in the areas where they are bought, there will be great shortages. Thus the unscrupulous greed of a few is ruining the very thing for which your island was once counted most fortunate. The high price of food is causing everyone to get rid of as many servants as possible, and what, I ask you, can they do but to beg, or, if more courageous, to rob?

"'What, moreover, is found alongside this wretched need and poverty but wanton luxury? For not only the servants of noblemen but craftsmen and farmers, indeed all classes alike, are given to flashy dress and fancy dining. Do not brothels, wine-shops, ale houses, and all those games of chance, cards, dicing, tennis, bowls, and quoits,[3] soon drain the purses of those who cannot resist them, sending them off to rob others when their money is gone? Cast out these ruinous plagues; make laws that those who have destroyed farmhouses and country

---

1   *murrain*   Infectious disease, usually of animals, especially sheep.
2   *oligopoly*   Control of prices by a handful of owners. Drawing on an analogy with "monopoly," More invents a word to satirize the landowners.
3   *quoits*   Game in which flat rings of stone, iron, or rope are pitched at a stake.

towns must either restore them or hand them over to those who will do so and are ready to build. Restrict this right of the rich to buy up everything and maintain a kind of monopoly. Let fewer be brought up in idleness. Let farming be restored. Let wool-manufacturing be reintroduced so that there may be honest occupations for the idle crowd of those whom poverty has already made thieves or who are currently vagabonds or lazy servants, and thus likely in any case to become such. Unless you remedy these evils, it is useless for you to boast of the justice you mete out in punishing theft. Such justice is for show, not truly fair or useful. For when you let your young be brought up badly, with their characters corrupted, and then penalize them when as adults they commit the very crimes that from their boyhood they had shown every prospect of committing, what else are you doing but first creating thieves and then punishing them?'"

"Even while I was speaking," Raphael said, "the lawyer had been preparing his reply, determined to adopt the usual method of disputants, who are more careful in repeating what has been said than in answering it, so highly do they regard memory.

"'Certainly, sir,' the lawyer said, 'you have spoken well, considering that you are but a stranger, and have been able only to hear something about these matters, not to get exact knowledge of them. I will briefly make things clear. First I will repeat in order what you have said; then I will show in what respects ignorance of our conditions has deceived you; finally I will demolish and destroy all your arguments. So to begin with what I promised first, in four respects you seemed to me—'

"'Hold your tongue,' said the Cardinal, interrupting the lawyer, 'for it looks as if your reply will be lengthy, if you begin thus.¹ We will relieve you of the trouble of making your answer now and postpone that duty until your next meeting, which I would like to schedule for tomorrow, if, of course, you are both free. But now I should very much like to hear, Raphael, your reasons why we should not punish theft with death. What penalty more beneficial to the commonweal would you recommend? For you must think some punishment is necessary. Even with the death penalty, men still rush into stealing. Give them a guarantee that they will live, then what force, what threat could deter the criminals? They would regard a lighter punishment as a reward, an invitation to commit more crime.'

---

1 [marginal note] Illustrates the Cardinal's way of interrupting a babbler.

"'Certainly,' I said to the Cardinal, 'most kind and reverend father, I think it quite unjust that what cost one person some money should cost another his life. Indeed, I do not think that all the goods in the world can equal a man's life in value. But some will say it is not about the money, but about the laws that have been assaulted, the justice that has been violated. They call this "extreme justice"—extreme wrong is more like it. For we ought not to approve such severe Manlian[1] laws that justify drawing the sword against even the slightest infraction. On the other hand, nor should we accept Stoical rulings that count all offences equal, so that there would be no difference between killing a man and taking his coin. If equity has any meaning, there is no similarity or connection between the two cases. God has said, "Thou shalt not kill," and shall we so lightly kill a man for taking a little money? And if the divine commandment does not stop us when we legalize killing, what prevents us from also legalizing adultery, rape and perjury? Now God forbids a man to take another's life—forbids him to take even his own. But certain men have mutually agreed to laws that do allow taking human life. If this exempts their agents from having to observe God's law, killing others without any divine example, will not human law then take precedent over that of God? And so men will obey God in the same way they manage everything else: as it suits them. Finally, the law of Moses, though severe and harsh (being made for an enslaved and stubborn people), nevertheless punishes theft by fine, not death. Let's not suppose that God's new law of mercy, in which He gives commands as a father to his children, allows us greater license to be cruel to one another. These are my reasons for thinking this treatment unlawful. Surely everyone knows how absurd and even dangerous to the commonwealth it is to penalize thief and a murderer with the same punishment. For as soon as a robber sees that he faces no more penalty for a murder conviction than for the mere guilt of theft, he would not hesitate to kill a man he might otherwise just rob. Because he is in no more danger if caught, it is safer for him to cover up the offence by making sure that there is no one left alive to tell the tale. And so even as we try to frighten thieves with excessive cruelty we also urge them on to the destruction of honest people.

---

1 *Manlian* Roman general Manlius (4th century BCE) executed his own son for breaking the law.

"'Now, as to determining what punishment might be better,' I continued to the Cardinal; 'that is an easy task. It would be much harder to find a worse! But why should we doubt the effectiveness of those punishments that worked for so long for the Romans, those experts in government? When men were convicted of great crimes they were condemned to a lifetime of working, shackled, in stone quarries or mines. Yet I can find no better custom in any nation than that which during my travels I noticed in Persia among the people commonly called the Polylerites.[1] Theirs is a large and well-governed nation. They pay an annual tribute to the Persian ruler, but they are in all other respects free and autonomous.[2] Living far from the sea, almost surrounded by mountains, and satisfied with what their own bounteous land yields, they neither visit others often nor receive visits. In accord with their ancient custom, they do not try to enlarge their territory. Their boundaries, moreover, are protected from all aggression by their mountains and by the tribute they pay to their overlord, and so they live free from military service, not at all extravagantly but comfortably, more in happiness than in fame or honor. Only their immediate neighbors even know their names.

"'In their land,' I went on, 'those who are convicted of theft repay what they have taken to the owner and, not, as is usual elsewhere, to the ruler, who they think has no more right to the stolen thing than do the thieves.[3] If the thing is lost, the value is made up and paid out of the thieves' belongings, the rest is given to their wives and children, and the thieves themselves are condemned to hard labor. Unless the theft was outrageous, they are neither shackled nor jailed but employed in public works, unbound and unguarded. If they refuse to work or if they slack off, they are whipped but not put in chains. If they do a good day's work, they need fear no humiliation. Every night after roll call, they are locked into their sleeping quarters. Aside from its constant toil, their life is not hard. As servants to the commonwealth, they are fed well at public expense, though the arrangement varies in different places. In some parts what is spent on them is raised by donations, and though this method is unpredictable, the people

---

1 *Polylerites* People of much nonsense, one of More's many invented Greek compounds: *polus* (much) and *leros* (nonsense).
2 [marginal note] The Polylerlite society near the Persians.
3 [marginal note] To be noted by us, who do otherwise.

are so kind hearted that the criminals' needs are plentifully supplied. Elsewhere public revenues are set aside to cover the cost, while in yet other places everyone pays a fixed tax. In some parts the offenders do no work for the community, but when someone needs a hired hand he can go to the marketplace and hire a convict for a day at a fixed wage that is less than what he would have had to pay a free man—and it is lawful to whip these servants if they become lazy. So the convicted thieves are never out of work, and beyond the cost of their keep each brings a little daily profit to the public treasury. They are all dressed in clothes of the same color,[1] with hair not shaved off but cropped a little above their ears and the tip of one ear cut off. Their friends may give them food, drink and the appropriately colored clothes, but it is a capital offence to give them money, both for the giver and the receiver. It is no less dangerous for a free man to receive money for any reason from one of these slaves, as the convicts are called, as it is for the slaves to touch weapons. A special badge distinguishes each district's slaves. It is a capital offence for slaves to throw away this badge, to go beyond their own bounds, or to talk to a slave from another district. And it is no less risky to plan an escape than actually to run away. Indeed, aiding and abetting an escape means death for a slave, and slavery for a free man. For an informer, however, there is a reward: money for a free man, liberty for a slave. Both are pardoned and given immunity for their help, thus ensuring that it is never safer to follow a wicked purpose than to repent it.

"'This is their way of arranging things,' I continued, 'as I have described it to you. You can easily see how humane and advantageous it is. The object of this punishment is to destroy the vice and save the person. The treatment of the criminals is necessary to make them good, and they have the rest of their lives to repair the damage they have done. There is so little fear of their backsliding that even travelers feel safe having these slaves as guides on their journeys, changing them for new ones as they arrive in new districts. Look, there are all sorts of obstacles to their committing a robbery: they are unarmed, money would simply betray them, penalties await them if caught, and there is absolutely no hope of escape. For how could a man expect to escape detection in clothes unlike those of anyone else in the country, unless he were to run away naked—and even then his ear would betray

---

1 [marginal note]   Yet modern servants exult in livery of the same sort.

him? It may be objected that convicts might get together and conspire against the state—as if any group of slaves could have a prayer without first tempting and persuading those of many other districts. But this could not happen, because they may not meet and converse, or even greet one another. It is unlikely that they would tell others of a plot when they know that plotting is dangerous if concealed but profitable to anyone who divulges it to the authorities. On the other hand, no one is quite without hope of some day recovering his liberty through obedience and patience, and by showing that he is capable of one day living a reformed life. For no year passes in which some are not restored to freedom, recommended by their patient endurance.'

"After saying this," Raphael continued, "I added that I saw no reason why this method might not also be adopted in England, and be more beneficial than the system of justice that my lawyerly opponent had praised so highly. The lawyer replied that it could never be established in England without seriously endangering the state. He shook his head, screwed up his face, and held his peace. And everyone there agreed with him. Then the Cardinal said, 'It is not easy to guess if it would turn out well without hazarding the attempt. But say a death penalty has been pronounced, and the King postpones its execution and suspends the right to sanctuary[1] in order to try this method. If the experiment works, it is only right to make it law. If it fails, putting to death those already condemned would be no less for the public good and no more unjust than to do so right away. In the meantime, no danger can come of the experiment. Moreover, I am sure that vagabonds might quite well be treated in the same way, for in spite of repeated legislation, we have not made much progress in dealing with them.'

"After the Cardinal said this, they all took turns praising the very plan they ridiculed when I suggested it. They were especially enthusiastic about the part concerning vagabonds, because it was the Cardinal's own addition.

"Perhaps it would be better to omit what followed, it was so absurd," said Raphael, "but I will relate it. It was not bad in itself and had some bearing on the matter.[2] There was present a hanger-on who

---

1   *right to sanctuary*   Right whereby criminals or those accused of crimes could demand asylum in churches, escaping—for a time at least—potential penalties imposed by law.
2   [marginal note]   The friar and the fool: a merry dialogue.

apparently wanted to adopt the role of fool, but what he said was too near the truth to be funny. His ill-timed jokes were meant to raise a laugh, but he himself was more often the object of laughter than were his jests. Sometimes the fellow made clever observations, however, thus confirming the proverb that if a man throws the dice often he will sooner or later get lucky. So it happened when one of the guests remarked that because my proposal provided well for thieves and the Cardinal had taken precautions for vagabonds, it remained only to make some provision for the poor, who were unable to earn a living because of sickness or old age.

"'Give me leave,' said the hanger-on, 'and I will see that this, too, is set right. For I am very anxious to get this sort of person out of my sight. They have often harassed me with their pitiful whinings, begging for money, but they could never pitch a tune that would get a coin out of my pocket. For one of two things always happens: either I do not want to give, or I cannot because I have nothing to give. So now they have begun to wise up, for when they see me pass by they say nothing, and spare their pains, expecting no more from me than they would from a priest.[1] But I would like to see a law that would distribute all those beggars among the Benedictine monasteries, where the men could become lay brothers,[2] as they call them, and the women could become nuns.'

"The Cardinal smiled and allowed it in jest. The others took it seriously—except for a certain friar, who was learned in theology. He was so delighted by this jest at the expense of priests and monks that he too began to laugh, though usually he was serious almost to the point of sourness.

"'Indeed,' said the friar,[3] 'you will not be rid of beggars, unless you make provision for us friars too.'

"'Already done,' said the hanger-on. 'His Eminence made excellent provision for you when he determined that vagabonds should be arrested and made to work. For you are the greatest vagabonds of all.'

---

1 [marginal note] A common saying of beggars.

2 *Benedictine monasteries* Monasteries of the Benedictine religious order, an order of monks founded in the sixth century by St. Benedict, notable for their influence on medieval education; *lay brothers* Men living and working in the monastery but who have not taken vows for clerical orders.

3 *friar* Member of one of the four mendicant orders—Franciscans, Dominicans, Carmelites, or Augustinians. Friars were not allowed private property, but instead begged or worked for their sustenance.

"After the company saw by looking at the Cardinal that he did not object to this joke any more than he had to the other, they all began to commend it vigorously. But not the friar, for he—and I do not wonder why—was stung by this taunt. He became so furious and enraged that he could not hold himself back from abuse. He called the man a rascal, a slanderer, a sneak, and a son of perdition, all the while quoting terrible denunciations out of Holy Scripture. Now the hanger-on began to laugh in earnest and was quite in his element.

"'Don't be angry, good friar,' he said, 'for it is written "In your patience ye shall possess your souls."'[1]

"To which the Friar replied—I will repeat his very words—'I am not angry, rogue, or at least I do not sin; for the Psalmist says, "Be ye angry, and sin not."'[2]

"Then the Cardinal gently cautioned the friar to calm himself, but he replied, 'No, my lord, I speak only from good zeal, as holy men should, as it says in the Scriptures, "The zeal of thy house hath consumed me," and we sing in Church—"The scorners of Elisha, while he went up to the house of God, felt the zeal[3] of the bald head,"[4] as perchance this vulgar scoffer shall feel it.'

"'Perhaps,' said the Cardinal, 'you mean well, but I think it would be wiser, though perhaps no holier, to keep from matching wits with a silly fellow or picking a foolish fight with a fool.'

"'No, my lord,' the friar said, 'it would not be wiser. As the wise Solomon saith, "Answer a fool according to his folly."[5] So I do now, and show him the pit into which he will fall, if he take not good heed. For if many scoffers at Elisha, who was only one bald head, felt the zeal of a bald head, how much more will be felt by one scorner of many friars, among whom are many bald men? Moreover, we have a Papal bull[6] by which all who scoff at us are excommunicated.'

---

1   *In your ... souls*   Luke 21.19.
2   [marginal note]   How his people speak in character! [*Be ye ... not* Psalms 4.4.]
3   [marginal note]   Out of ignorance, the friar uses "zelus" as if it were a neuter noun, like "scelus." [In the original Latin, the friar incorrectly says "zelus" instead of "zelum," using the wrong form of the noun.]
4   *The zeal ... me*   Psalms 69.9;   *The scorners ... bald head*   In 2 Kings 2.23–24, Elisha, the heir of the prophet Elijah, curses a group of children who have mocked his baldness. Two bears attack the children, killing forty-two of them.
5   *Solomon*   King of Israel noted for his wisdom;   *Answer a ... folly*   Proverbs 26.5.
6   *Papal bull*   Decree issued by the Pope, so called because it was closed by a lead *bulla*, or seal.

"When the Cardinal saw there was no end to the matter in sight, he dismissed the hanger-on with a motion of his head and turned the conversation to a more suitable subject. Soon afterwards he rose from table, dismissed us, and went to hear what the petitioners[1] had to say.

"There, Master More," concluded Raphael, "what a long tale I have burdened you with, one that I would never have told at such length if you had not in the first place so eagerly pestered me and then listened as if you did not want me to leave out a thing. I could have told it more briefly, but I had to tell it in every point to show the judgment of those who initially rejected what I said but then immediately supported it when the Cardinal did not disapprove. They flattered him so much that they even encouraged and almost took in earnest the suggestions of the hanger-on, which the Cardinal took as a joke. So from this you may judge how little regard courtiers would pay me and my advice."

"To be sure, Raphael," I said, "you have given me great pleasure, so wise and clever is everything you have said. Besides, while listening to you I felt not only as if I were at home in my native country, but also as if I had gone back to the days of my youth, for I was pleasantly reminded of the Cardinal in whose household I was brought up as a boy. And since you so highly honor his memory, you cannot think how much more attached I am to you for that than I was already. But my mind is still not changed, and I continue to think that if you could persuade yourself not to shun the courts of kings, you could do the greatest good to the commonwealth through your advice. This is the most important part of your duty, as it that of every good man. For since your favorite writer, Plato, believes that states will be happy only if philosophers are kings or kings turn to philosophy, what a faint hope there will be of happiness if philosophers will not share their advice with kings."[2]

"Philosophers are not so ungracious," Raphael said, "as to refuse to advise monarchs—indeed, many have done so through published books. But rulers must be ready to take good advice. Doubtless Plato was right that unless kings become philosophical they will never take the advice of real philosophers. From their youth, most are infected by and saturated with wrong ideas. Plato experienced this with

---

1   *petitioners* Those asking for favors from the Church authorities.
2   *For since ... kings* See Plato's *Republic* 5.473.

Dionysius.[1] So if I were to give wise advice to some king, trying to remove the seeds of evil and corruption from his mind, do you not think that as a result, I would be at once banished or ridiculed?

"Come now, imagine me at the French king's court, sitting with the most trusted members of his Privy Council. Imagine the king presiding as they all set their wits to determine by what crafty means he might keep his hold on Milan, bring Naples (which has for the time eluded his grasp) back into his power, destroy Venice, subjugate the whole of Italy, and then add to his rule Flanders, Brabant and the whole of Burgundy, as well as other lands.[2] And suppose that someone advises that he should sign a treaty with the Venetians meant to last only so long as he thought convenient, and that he should develop a common strategy with them, even allowing them to keep part of the booty, which, when all has gone as he wished, he could reclaim. While one counselor recommends the hiring of German lanzknechts,[3] another suggests winning over the Swiss with money,[4] and a third advises appeasing the offended majesty of the Emperor with gold. A fourth thinks that a settlement should be made with the King of Aragon, to whom the independent kingdom of Navarre would be ceded as a guarantee of peace, while still another proposes that the king of Castile should be lured by the prospect of a marriage alliance and that the offer of money would draw some Castilian nobles over to the French side.

"The most perplexing question is what to do with England. The advisers agree that peace should be made and that the alliance, which may be weak at first, should be strengthened as much as possible so that the English could be called friends and suspected as enemies. The Scots therefore must be posted in readiness, ready for any opportunity to be let loose on the English should the latter make any move. Moreover, some exiled noble must be encouraged (secretly, for treaties prevent this being done openly) to maintain a claim to the throne so that he may keep in check a king he does not trust.

"In a case like this, with such plans afoot and each vying with the other in making warlike proposals, what do you suppose would hap-

---

1 *Dionysius* Dionysus II, tyrant of Syracuse (c. 397–343 BCE). Plato unsuccessfully attempted to instruct him in philosophy.
2 [marginal note] Indirectly he discourages the French from seizing Italy.
3 *lanzknechts* German infantry (literally "lance knights").
4 [marginal note] Swiss mercenaries.

pen if an insignificant person like myself got up and advised another tack: leave Italy alone and stay at home, for as it is, the kingdom of France is almost too large to be well governed by a single man, and so the king should not think of adding another dominion. Suppose I then put before them the decisions taken by the Achorians,[1] who live on the mainland southeast of the Island of Utopia?[2] They went to war to win their king another kingdom, one he claimed because of an old marriage alliance. After securing it they saw it would take no less trouble to keep it than it had taken to obtain it, for there were constant rebellions and foreign invasions. So the Achorians had to keep an army in constant readiness, either to defend them or in case of an attack by them. In the meantime they were being plundered, money was leaving the country, they were losing their lives for the glory of others, and peace was no more secure than before. War corrupted their citizens' morals and they developed a lust for robbery and murder, holding laws in contempt because the king, distracted by governing two kingdoms, could not properly attend to either. Eventually, seeing no other way to end this mischief, the Achorians rallied together and courteously but firmly offered their king his choice of whichever kingdom he preferred. He could not keep both because each had too many people to be ruled by half a king. For who would hire a mule-driver if he worked half the time for somebody else? So the worthy king was forced to be content with his own realm. He handed over the new one to one of his friends, who was soon afterwards driven out.

"Furthermore, imagine I proved that all this warfare, by which so many nations would be kept in turmoil on the French king's account, would, after draining his resources and destroying his people, come to nothing in the end. So it would be more beneficial for him to look after his own kingdom and make it as rich and as flourishing as possible: loving his subjects, being loved by them, living with them, and ruling them gently with no designs upon other kingdoms since what he has is more than enough for him. Now what reception, friend More, do you think this advice of mine would find?"

---

1 *Achorians*   People with no country; another invented Greek compound: *a* (without) and *xoros* (country).
2 [marginal note]   A notable example.

"To be sure, not a very favorable one," I said.

"Well, then, let us proceed," he said. "Suppose the King and his counselors are debating and calculating how they might heap up treasure for him. One advises raising the value of money when he has to pay off debts and lowering it when he has to receive any. Thus he could settle a large debt with a small sum but receive a large one when only a small one is due him. Another suggests a make-believe war as a pretext for raising money. Then when he saw fit, he could make peace with great solemnity, misleading the people into believing that their king was compassionate, eagerly avoiding bloodshed. Another reminds him of old moth-eaten laws that no one remembers and so everyone has broken. He could exact fines for such infractions, there being no better source of profit—nor any more honorable, for such an approach can outwardly resemble justice. Another says that the king should prohibit many common activities under threat of heavy fines, and then, for large sums of money, allow exceptions to those whose interests are hampered by the prohibition. Thus favor is won from the people, and a double profit is made, first by the exaction of fines from those whose greed has entangled them in the snare, and then by selling privileges to others at a higher price. In fact, the higher the price the better the prince: since he dislikes making exceptions harmful to the common welfare, he will not do so except for much money.

"Another counselor persuades him that he must befriend judges who always decide in favor of the royal prerogative. He must summon them to the palace and invite them to debate his affairs in his presence. In even the most unfair of charges, the judges will all, from a desire to contradict, to be original, or to win favor, find some loophole whereby a false accusation may be set up. If the judges can be made to differ, even the clearest claim will need to be debated and truth becomes a matter of doubt. A convenient handle will be given to the king to interpret the law in his own interest, and everyone else will acquiesce from shame or fear. The sentence will boldly be pronounced from the Bench, and then a pretext can never be lacking for deciding for the king. To such a judge it is enough to have on his side either the letter of the law, or a twisted reading of it, or (what outweighs all law with conscientious judges) the undoubted prerogative of the King's majesty.

"Thus all the counselors agree, consenting to the saying of Crassus:[1] no amount of gold is enough for a king who must keep an army.[2] A king, however much he might want to, can do nothing wrong, for all that men possess is his—they themselves are his—and a man's own is only what the king's generosity does not take away. It is much to the king's interest to leave him as little as possible, so that the people do not threaten him by growing wanton with riches and freedom. Freedom and riches would make them less willing to endure harsh and unjust commands, whereas poverty and need depress them, encouraging their patience and taking away from the oppressed the lively spirit of rebellion.

"Suppose again I rose and maintained that this advice was both dishonorable and dangerous for the king, whose very safety, as well as his honor, rested on the people's resources and not on his own. Suppose I argued that people choose their king for their own sake and not for his, that he has a duty to ensure that they live well, safe from injustice and wrong. That it is the king's responsibility to take more care for the welfare of his people than for his own, just as it is the duty of a shepherd, insofar as he is a shepherd, to feed his flock rather than himself.[3] That whoever thinks the stability of the kingdom rests in the poverty of the people is way off the mark, proved wrong by the facts. For where do you see more quarrelling than among beggars? Who is more eager for revolution than a man discontented with his state of life? Who is more reckless in upsetting order in the hope of profiting by any means or other than someone with nothing to lose? Now if there was a king so despised and hated by his subjects, that the only way he could maintain order would be to oppress, plunder, and harass them, and so reduce them to poverty, it would surely be better for him to resign his throne than to keep it by such means. Otherwise, though he might retain the name of ruler he loses its majesty. For it is not a king's part to reign over beggars, but rather over the prosper-

---

1 *Crassus* Roman statesman (d. 53 BCE) who—along with Caesar and Pompey—made up the first triumvirate. According to Cicero, Crassus said that only those who had the money to maintain an army should take part in government.
2 [marginal note]   Saying of Crassus the Rich.
3 *That it is ... himself* See Plato's *Republic* 1.343, which argues that the true ruler always acts in his subjects' best interest, not his own. Also see Aristotle's *Politics* 4.8.3, which defines a tyrant as one who rules with his own private interests in mind, rather than those of his people.

ous and happy. This was certainly the opinion of that noble and lofty spirit Fabricius,[1] who said that he would rather rule rich men than be rich himself.

"If one man lives a life of pleasure and self-indulgence amidst the groans and lamentations of all around him, he is the keeper of a prison, not of a kingdom. Just as a doctor who cannot cure one disease except by creating another must admit he is incompetent, so a monarch who cannot correct the lives of citizens except by depriving them of the good things of life must admit that he does not know how to govern free men.

"Such a king should rule his own self-indulgence or pride, for it is generally as a result of these vices that the people either scorn or hate him. Let him live harmlessly on what is his own and limit his expenses to his revenues. Let him put a stop to evildoers, and by training his subjects well prevent new evils rather than allow them to develop and then have to punish them. Let him not be hasty in putting into force laws long since fallen into disuse, especially those that were never needed.[2] And let him never confiscate property that no judge would allow a private person to appropriate; it would be crafty and unjust to act that way.

"What if I then recommended to them a law of the Macarians,[3] a people not very far from Utopia? Their king, on the day he first takes office, after solemn sacrifices, is bound by an oath that he will never have in his treasury more than a thousand pounds of gold, or its equivalent in silver.[4] They say that this law was instituted by an excellent king who cared more for his country's good than for his own wealth; his aim was to prevent any ruler from hoarding so much money that he would impoverish his people. He saw that his present wealth was enough to quell a rebellion or defend the kingdom against invasion but not large enough to tempt him to invade the lands of others. This was the law's main purpose; it also provided sufficient funds for daily transactions with the citizenry. Finally, a king who has to pay out to the people whatever exceeds the limit prescribed by

---

1   *Fabricius*   Roman general and statesman (d. 275 BCE), noted for his incorruptibility.
2   *Let him ... needed*   Some counselors to Henry VII were notorious for fining citizens for breaking laws so old they did not know of their existence.
3   *Macarians*   "Happy ones," from the Greek *makarios* (blessed or happy).
4   [marginal note]   Wonderful law of the Macarians.

law, he is less likely to oppress them. Such a king will be a terror to the evil and be loved by the good. But if I tried to tell these truths to men strongly inclined to the opposite way of thinking, would I not be telling my tale to deaf ears?"[1]

"Deaf indeed, without a doubt," I said, "and by Heaven I am not surprised. Nor, to tell the truth, do I think such talk should be thrust on people, nor such advice given to those who will never listen to it. What good could such novel ideas do? How could they penetrate minds of those entirely possessed by the opposite view? In private conversation among friends this academic sort of philosophizing is not without its charm, but in the councils of kings, where great matters are debated with great authority, there is no room for such things."

"That is just what I meant," he said, "by saying there is no room for philosophy in dealing with kings."

"Yes there is," I said, "but not for this academic philosophy that thinks every thing suited to every place.[2] There is another philosophy, however, a practical one better suiting political life, one that knows its cues, adapts itself to them, and in the play at hand performs its own part neatly and fittingly. This is the one you must use.[3] Suppose a comedy of Plautus is being performed, and just as the household slaves are making trivial jokes at each other you come on the stage in a philosopher's getup and spoke those lines from the *Octavia* in which Seneca is arguing with Nero. Would it not be better to have a non-speaking part than to recite something inappropriate and thus mangle a perfectly good comedy?[4] You spoil and unbalance the play by bringing in irrelevant matter, even if your own lines are superior. Whatever drama is being staged, perform it as well as you can and don't try to wreck it just because you think of another that has more charm.

"So it is in the commonwealth and in the deliberations of kings. Suppose wrong opinions cannot be pulled up by the root and that you cannot cure, as you would wish, vices of long standing. You must

---

1 [marginal note]   Proverb.

2 [marginal note]   Philosophy of the Schools.

3 [marginal note]   A striking comparison.

4 *Plautus*   Roman playwright (c. 254–184 BCE) known for his low-brow, farcical comedies; *Octavia*   Grave play in the tragic historical mode, spuriously attributed to Seneca; *comedy* [marginal note]   A mute part.

not on that account abandon the ship of state during a storm just because you cannot control the winds. Neither must you try to impose upon ministers of state strange and untested notions that you know will carry no weight with those of opposite conviction. You must do your best with an indirect approach and with covert suggestions. And when you cannot ensure a good outcome you must make it as little bad as you can. It is impossible that all can be well until all people are entirely good, something I do not expect for a great many years to come."

"By such means," Raphael said, "I would accomplish nothing except to share the madness of others while attempting to cure their lunacy. If I wish to speak the truth, I must do so in the manner I have described. For all I know, it may be the role of a philosopher to speak falsely, but it is not mine. Although my language may be unwelcome and disagreeable, I cannot see why it should seem so strange that they would think me foolish. It's not as if I told them the kind of things that Plato imagines in his *Republic*, or that the Utopians actually put in practice in theirs.[1] Though such institutions might seem superior (as in fact they are) they might also seem bizarre, because here we have private property, whereas there everything is held in common.

"My advice, in that case, would surely not be accepted—not only because it would be addressed to those who had made up their minds to go headlong down the opposite path, but also because people tend to resent it. But leaving that aside, what have I recommended that would not be appropriate or desirable everywhere? Truly, if all things that to the perverse ways of humanity have come to seem peculiar must be dismissed as unusual and absurd, we must also suppress almost all the doctrines of Christ. And He forbade us to suppress them—so much so that what He whispered in the ears of His disciples, He ordered them to proclaim openly from the housetops.[2] The greater part of His teaching is far more alien to our customary ways than anything I said. But preachers, crafty men that they are, and I suppose following your advice, found that people did not wish to change their ways so as to fit the words of Christ, and so they adapted them to human behavior as if His were a rule of lead, not of iron, in the hope that somehow the two might be reconciled. I cannot

---

1 [marginal note] Utopian institutions.
2 *what He ... housetops* See Matthew 10.27 and Luke 12.3.

see what they have gained except to allow us to be bad with a good conscience. I would achieve no more in the councils of kings. Either I would offer a different opinion, which would be overruled, or I would voice the same opinion as the others, in which case I would, like Mitio in Terence,[1] share their madness. As to the indirect approach you suggested, saying that if all things cannot be made good, they must at least be so handled as to be made, as far as can be done, as little bad as possible, I do not see the use. At court there is no room for dissembling, nor can you shut your eyes to things; you must openly approve the worst advice, and subscribe to the most ruinous decrees. He will be counted as a spy, almost a traitor, who even stutters in his praise of evil advice. Moreover, you have no chance to do any good when you mix with colleagues more likely to corrupt the best of men than to be reformed. Their evil conversation will either seduce you or turn your integrity and innocence into a screen for the wickedness and folly of others. Thus you are far from being able to make anything better by your indirect approach and your covert suggestions.

"For this reason, Plato shows in a wonderful analogy why philosophers are right to stay away from political life. Although they observe people rushing into the streets and getting soaked by constant showers, they cannot induce them to come in out of the rain. Knowing that they will accomplish nothing by going out, other than to get soaked with the rest, they stay put under cover, content that though they cannot cure the stupidity of others, they can at least save their own heads.[2]

"My dear More, to speak frankly from the heart, it seems to me that wherever you have private property, and all men measure all things by money, it is scarcely possible to have justice or prosperity. Surely you don't think there is justice when all good things come into the hands of the worst people, or that there is prosperity where a very few own everything. Even then those few are not fully content, while the many are downright wretched.

"Consider the wise and holy institutions of the Utopians, among whom, and with very few laws, affairs are so well ordered that virtue

---

1   *Mitio*   Character in a comedy (*The Brothers*) by Terence (c. 190–158 BCE), a Roman playwright. In the speech referred to here, Mitio declares, "Still, if I inflamed or even fell in with his passionate temper, I should surely give him another madman for company" (1.145–47).

2   *Plato ... their own heads*   See *Republic* 6.469 D-E.

is rewarded and yet everyone has an equal abundance of everything. Contrast this with the situation of those many nations that keep creating fresh laws yet never manage to create good order—states in which whatever a man has grabbed he calls his own property but in which all these laws still do not help him secure or defend his goods or distinguish them from those of others (and notice the ever rising number of interminable lawsuits in such nations over what belongs to whom). I tell you, when I consider all this I become more partial to Plato and understand why he disdained to make laws for those who refused to accept the principle of granting an equal share of good things to everyone.[1] The wise philosopher foresaw that the one and only road to the general welfare of a commonwealth would be to enforce equality in all respects.

"I doubt that such well being could be achieved where there is private property. For when everyone aims to have as much of it as possible, even where there is a great wealth it is divvied up among a few, who leave nothing to the rest but poverty. And it generally happens that one class deserves the lot of the other, for the rich tend to be greedy, unscrupulous and useless, while the poor tend to be well behaved, simple and useful—more useful, by their daily labor, to the community than to themselves. I am entirely convinced that no just and even distribution of goods can be made, nor any perfect happiness be found among human beings, until private property is utterly abolished. While it lasts, for most of mankind, and not the worst, there will remain a heavy and intolerable burden of poverty and anxiety. I admit that this can be relieved to some extent, but I maintain that it cannot be removed. A statute might be made that no one be allowed to hold more than a certain amount of land, and that no one might have an income beyond a certain maximum. Laws could be passed to prevent the king from becoming too powerful and the people from becoming arrogant. There might also be legislation to stop public offices from being bought and sold, or held only at great personal expense. Otherwise, officials might take the chance to recoup by fraud and robbery what they spent to gain office, and then the rich would hold offices that should be held by the wise. Laws such as these can alleviate and lessen these evils, just as sick bodies that are

---

1 *he refused ... everyone* This was Plato's reason for refusing to rule the Arcadians and the Thebans when the possibility was offered to him.

past cure can still be kept going by constant medical treatment. There is no hope of a cure or a return to health, however, while each man is master of his own property. Indeed, while you are occupied with the curing of one part, you make the sores of the other worse; thus the disease of the one arises from the healing of the other, since nothing can be added to one man without being subtracted from another."

"I can't agree," I said. "Life can never be happy or satisfying where all things are held in common. How could a sufficient supply of goods be kept up? Each person would spend less time working. If hope of personal gain does not motivate a man, he becomes lazy and relies on the industry of others. But when people are driven to labor by poverty and are not allowed to keep what they have worked for, is there not bound to be continual trouble, bloodshed, and revolution? Not to mention that magistrates must lose both authority and dignity, for how there can be any place for them among men who are all on the same level escapes me."

"I am not surprised that you think so," Raphael said, "for you have either have no conception, or a false one, of the sort of state I describe. If you had been with me in Utopia and had yourself seen how people behave, as I did (for I lived there more than five years, and would never have wished to leave except for the desire to make that new world widely known), you certainly would admit that you had never seen a more well-ordered people anywhere."

"Yet surely," said Peter Giles, "it will be hard for you to convince me that one might find in that new world a people better ordered than in our own familiar one. I imagine our governments are older and our minds at least equal in intelligence. Long experience has helped us to invent many conveniences for human life, not to speak of the things we discovered by pure luck and that no amount of intelligence could have devised."

"As for the age of states," said Raphael, "you could give a better opinion if you had read the world's histories; if we may believe them, there were cities there before there were men here. As to what intelligence has invented or chance discovered, that might have happened equally in both places. But even if it's true that we surpass the Utopians in intelligence, I am sure they leave us far behind in perseverance and industry. For according to their chronicles, up to our arrival they had never heard anything about us, whom they call the *Ultraequinoctials*, except that 1,200 years ago a ship driven by tempests to the island of Utopia was wrecked there. Some Romans and Egyptians were cast on shore and never left the island. Now mark with what industry they exploited this one opportunity. There was no useful art in the Roman empire that the Utopians did not either learn from the shipwrecked strangers or discover themselves after making some inquiries. What advantage they took of the chance arrival of a few men there! But if the same fortune has ever carried someone from their country to ours, it is completely forgotten, as perhaps it will be forgotten in times to come that I was ever at Utopia. At our first encounter they immediately took up any good invention of ours, yet I suppose it will be a long time before we receive and adopt anything that is better ordered by them. This, I think, is the chief reason why, though we are inferior to them neither in intelligence nor in wealth, their commonwealth is more wisely governed and more prosperous than ours."

"Well, Raphael," I said, "I insist that you give us a description of the island, and do not be brief, but set forth in order the land, the rivers, the cities, the inhabitants, the manners, customs and laws— in fact everything that you think we would like to know. And you may imagine we'd like to know everything of which we are as yet ignorant."

"There is nothing," he said, "I would be more pleased to do, for I have the facts ready to hand. But it will take time."

"Then," I said, "let us go in to dinner, and afterwards we will take up as much time as we like."

"So be it," he said.

So we went in and dined, and then returned to the same spot, sat down on the same bench, and having given orders to the servants that we must not be interrupted, Peter Giles and I urged Raphael to fulfill his promise. When he saw us intent and eager to listen, after sitting in silent thought for a time, he thus began his tale.

Book 2

Chapter 1
The Geography of Utopia

The island of Utopia extends in the center (where it is broadest) for two hundred miles, and this breadth continues for the greater part of the island, but towards both ends it begins gradually to taper.[1] These ends form a circuit of about 500 miles, so that the island resembles a new moon with horns divided by a strait about eleven miles across that then opens out into a wide expanse. The land that almost surrounds the bay keeps the winds off the water, making it seem like a huge lake, unruffled and not subject to storms. Thus almost all the center of the island makes a harbor, one in which ships can go in every direction to the great convenience of the inhabitants. Shallows and rocks make the mouth of this sea (which is situated between the horns) dangerous. Near the center of the gap stands one great cliff, which is not dangerous because clearly visible. On it stands a tower, manned by a garrison.[2] The other rocks are hidden, and therefore treacherous. Only the natives know the channels, so very few foreigners enter the gulf without a Utopian pilot. Even for them the entrance is hardly safe, but they are guided by landmarks on the shore. If these were removed and resituated, the shoals could easily destroy an enemy fleet, however large.[3]

On the opposite coast there are numerous harbors, but the landing is everywhere so well defended by nature or by art that it would take only a few men to prevent a strong force from invading. As is recorded, and as the appearance of the ground shows, the island was not surrounded by sea until the time of Utopus, who conquered it and gave it its name (up to then it was called "Abraxa").[4] He brought a rude and rustic people to such a degree of civilization and refinement that they now excel almost all others. After a victory on his first landing, he ordered the land excavated for fifteen miles where it was connected to the mainland, thus letting the sea flow round it.[5]

---

1 [marginal note] Site and shape of Utopia and the new island.
2 [marginal note] Being naturally safe, the entry is defended by a single fort.
3 [marginal note] The trick of shifting landmarks.
4 [marginal note] Utopia named for King Utopia.
5 [marginal note] This was a bigger job than digging across the Isthmus. [Several unsuccessful attempts had been made to dig a canal across the Isthmus of Corinth, which joins

He set to the task not only the inhabitants but his own soldiers, and so he prevented anyone from thinking the task imposed upon him a disgrace. By dividing the work equally among so many hands, he ensured that it was finished with astonishing speed. The neighbors, who had at first ridiculed the undertaking as vain, were struck with wonder and terror at his success.[1] The island contains 54 cities or county towns, all large and fine, identical in language, manners, customs and laws,[2] similar in situation, and everywhere, so far as the nature of the ground permits, the same in appearance.[3] None of them is less than twenty-four miles from the next, but none is so isolated that you cannot go from it to another in a day's journey on foot.[4] From each city three senior and experienced citizens meet once a year at Amaurote,[5] the capital, to discuss affairs of common interest to the island, for the city's central location makes it the most conveniently situated place to which representatives of all parts can travel.

The land is so well distributed that each city has at least twenty miles of it on every side, and on some sides more, where the towns are farther apart.[6] No town has any desire to extend its territory, for its citizens consider themselves to be cultivators, not owners, of what they hold.[7] Everywhere in the country they have provided, at suitable distances from each other, farmhouses well equipped with farming tools.[8] These are inhabited by citizens who come in succession to live there. No rural household numbers fewer than forty men and women, besides two slaves attached to the soil, and over each are set a responsible master and mistress of mature years. A Phylarch[9] rules over every thirty households. Twenty from each household return every year to the city, after completing two years in the country. In their place the same number are sent fresh from the city to be instructed by those who have already been there a year and are therefore more

the Peloponnesian peninsula to the rest of Greece. As a result of these repeated failures, this was a proverbially difficult task.]

1 [marginal note]   Many hands make light work.

2 [marginal note]   The towns of Utopia.

3 [marginal note]   Likeness breeds concord.

4 [marginal note]   A middling distance between towns.

5 *Amaurote*   Dim or dark; from the Greek *amauroton*, meaning "made dark."

6 [marginal note]   Distribution of land.

7 [marginal note]   But today this is the curse of all countries.

8 [marginal note]   Farming is the prime occupation.

9 *Phylarch*   Leader of the tribe, from the Greek *phylarchos*, meaning "head of a group."

experienced in husbandry. They themselves teach others the following year; so there is no danger of any mistake or ineptitude causing scarcity, as might happen if all at one time were newcomers without knowledge of husbandry.

Though this system of changing the cultivators of the soil is the rule, designed to prevent anyone being forced to continue long in a life of hard work, men who take a natural pleasure in agriculture can obtain leave to stay several years. The job of the cultivator is to till the ground, to feed the animals, and to get wood, getting it to town by land or water, as is most convenient.[1] Cultivators breed a great quantity of poultry by a wonderful device.[2] The hens do not sit on the eggs; instead, a great number of eggs are kept at a uniform heat until they come to life and hatch. As soon as they have come out of the shell, the chicks follow and recognize human beings instead of hens. They breed very few horses and these only high-spirited ones, which they use for no other purpose than to exercise their young men in horsemanship.[3] All the labor of cultivation and transport is performed by oxen, which may be inferior to horses in a sprint, but are far superior to them in staying power and endurance and not susceptible to so many diseases.[4] Moreover, it takes less trouble and expense to feed them, and when they are past work can be eaten.

Utopians grow grain only for bread.[5] They drink wine, made of grapes or of apples and pears, or else pure water infused with honey or licorice, which they have in abundance.[6] Though they know for certain how much grain the city and its adjacent lands require, they produce far more grain and cattle than they need and distribute the surplus among their neighbors.[7] Whenever they require anything not found in the country, they requisition it from the city, and without having to give anything in exchange easily obtain it from the town officials and have it brought to them every month on a recurring holiday, when many people go to the city and can help transport the needed materials. When the time of harvest is at hand, the Phylarchs

---

1 [marginal note] Farmers' jobs.
2 [marginal note] A notable way of hatching eggs.
3 [marginal note] Uses of the horse.
4 [marginal note] Uses of oxen.
5 *Utopians ... bread* Rather than for making ale or beer.
6 [marginal note] Food and drink.
7 [marginal note] Planned planting.

in the country tell the city officials how many citizens they need. These harvesters, arriving at the appointed time, and weather permitting, complete almost all the harvest work in a single day.[1]

Chapter 2
The Cities, and Especially Amaurote

If you know one of the cities, you know them all, for as far as the landscape permits they are almost identical, so I could describe this one or that—it does not matter which I would choose—but nothing could be better than Amaurote.[2] None is worthier, for the others defer to it as the place where the Council meets; and none is better known to me, for I lived there for a full five years.

Built on the gentle slope of a hill, Amaurote is almost square-shaped. Its breadth is about two miles starting from just below the crest of the hill and running down to the river Anyder;[3] its length along the river is rather more than its breadth.[4] The river, which rises eighty miles beyond Amaurote from a small spring, is augmented by various tributaries, two of which are fairly large, so that by the time it reaches the city it is half a mile across. It becomes even broader as it flows a further sixty miles and then falls into the ocean. Through the whole distance between the city and the sea, and even above the city for some miles, the tide flows in rapidly for six hours at a time and then recedes with equal speed. When the sea comes in it fills the whole bed of the Anyder with its water for a distance of thirty miles and drives the river back.[5] At such times it turns its water salt for some distance farther, but after that the river becomes gradually fresh and passes the city untainted. When the ebb comes, the fresh water extends almost down to the mouth of the river.

Amaurote is joined to the opposite bank of the river not by a wooden bridge but by a stone one with fine arches.[6] It is placed at the corner of the city farthest from the sea so that sea-going ships may easily pass along almost the whole town. There is also another

---

1 [marginal note] The value of collective labor.
2 [marginal note] Description of Amaurote, first city of Utopia.
3 *Anyder* Without water, from the Greek *anydros*, meaning "waterless."
4 [marginal note] The river Anyder.
5 [marginal note] Just like the Thames in England.
6 [marginal note] Here too London is just like Amaurote.

river, not large but very gentle and pleasant, which rises out of the same hill on which the town is built and flows through it into the Anyder. The Amaurotians have fortified the source of this river with walls connecting it to the city so that no invading enemy can divert or pollute their drinking water.[1] From where it enters, the water is distributed by brick channels into various parts of the lower town. Where the ground makes that impossible, rainwater collected in big cisterns serves the purpose. A high and broad wall with many towers and battlements surrounds the town.[2] A ditch, dry but deep, broad, and made impassable by thorn hedges, surrounds the walls on three sides; on the fourth side is the river.

The streets are well laid out both for traffic and to avoid the winds.[3] The houses, which are in no way shabby, are set together in long continuous rows facing one another, with twenty-foot wide streets in between.[4] Behind the houses, along the whole length of each street, lies a broad garden enclosed on all sides.[5] Every house has not only a door onto the street but also a back door into the garden. Folding doors, opening easily by hand and closing automatically, give admission to anyone, so that nothing at all is private.[6] Indeed, every ten years citizens exchange their houses by lot. Utopians are very fond of their gardens. These have vines, fruits, herbs, and flowers, so well kept and flourishing that I had never seen anything so fruitful or elegant. They take great pleasure in the gardens themselves but also in keen competition among streets as to which block will have the best ones. Certainly you cannot find anything in the whole city more profitable and enjoyable to the citizens, and there was nothing that the first founder cared more for than these gardens.[7]

They say that Utopus himself first laid out the whole city but left its adornment and improvement to future generations, knowing that there was too much to be done in one lifetime. According to their chronicles (which cover 1,760 years of history and are most carefully preserved), their first houses were low, mere hovels and cabins with

---

1 [marginal note] A source of drinking water.
2 [marginal note] City walls.
3 [marginal note] Streets, of what sort.
4 [marginal note] Buildings.
5 [marginal note] Gardens next to the houses.
6 [marginal note] This smacks of Plato's community.
7 [marginal note] Virgil also wrote in praise of gardens. [See *Georgics*, 4.16–48.]

mud walls and thatched roofs. But now all the houses are handsome, with three stories and walls faced by flint, plaster, or brick. The roofs are flat and covered with a cement that is inexpensive yet so well mixed that it is fire-resistant and better than lead in resisting the violence of storms. Utopians keep the wind out of their windows by glass, which is in very common use, or sometimes by thin cloth smeared with translucent oil or amber. This has two advantages: more light is let in, and the winds are better kept out.[1]

Chapter 3
The System of Local Government

Each year every thirty families choose a representative whom in their old language they had called a "Syphogrant"[2] but now call a "Phylarch."[3] Over every ten Syphogrants with their families is set a Tranibor,[4] or chief Phylarch. Then the whole body of two hundred Syphogrants, having sworn to pick the one best qualified for the position, chooses by secret ballot a chief executive from four candidates nominated by the citizens[5] in each quarter of the city.

The chief governor holds office for life unless suspected of trying to make himself a dictator.[6] The Tranibors are elected annually and are not changed without good reason, but other administrators hold office for one year. The Tranibors consult the governor every other day, more often if need be. They discuss the affairs of the commonwealth, and if there are disputes between private persons—which happen rarely—they settle them quickly.[7] Each day the Tranibors invite two different Syphogrants into the chamber. Nothing concerning the commonwealth may be ratified unless it has been discussed by the Senate on three different days,[8] and talking about public affairs outside the Senate or the electoral body is a capital offence. These

---

1 [marginal note]   Windows of glass or oiled linen.
2 *Syphogrant*   Wiseman, from the Greek *sophos* (wise) and *gerontes* (old men).
3 [marginal note]   In the Utopian tongue "tranibor" means "chief official."
4 *Tranibor*   Plain-glutton, from the Greek *tranos* (plain, clear) and *boros* (devouring, gluttonous).
5 [marginal note]   A notable way of electing officials.
6 [marginal note]   Tyranny hateful to the well-ordered commonwealth.
7 [marginal note]   A quick ending to disputes, which now are endlessly and deliberately prolonged.
8 [marginal note]   No abrupt decisions.

rules, Utopians say, make it harder for governor and Tranibors to plot a tyranny and change the nature of the commonwealth. And so important matters are referred to the assembly of Syphogrants, who after informing their families confer and then report their decision to the Senate. Sometimes the matter is laid before the council of the whole island. By custom, the Senate postpones debate on a new matter until the next day, so that no one will blurt out what first comes into his mind and then put all his effort into defending what he had said rather than into thinking of the commonweal, willing to sacrifice the public good if he might save his reputation from seeming to have had so little foresight. He should have taken care at the outset to speak with wisdom rather than in haste.[1]

Chapter 4
Crafts and Occupations

Agriculture is the one pursuit common to all, both men and women, without exception.[2] Everyone is trained in it from early years, partly in school and partly by being taken for an outing to the nearby farmland, where students don't just watch but get their exercise by lending a hand.

Besides agriculture, which as I said is common to all, each person is taught some craft, generally wool working, preparing linen, masonry, carpentry, blacksmith's work, or silk weaving.[3] No other pursuit occupies very many people.[4] Each family makes its own clothes, which are in the same style throughout the island except for distinctions between the sexes and between the married and the single.[5] The garments please the eye, allow the body to move easily, and suit both summer and winter. Everyone, man and woman alike, learns one of these crafts.[6] But women, the weaker sex, take on the lighter tasks, generally working with wool and linen, while the men do the heavy

---

1 [marginal note] This is the old saying, "Do your thinking overnight."
2 [marginal note] Agriculture is everyone's business, though now we put it off on a despised few.
3 *Besides ... weaving* In contrast to Plato's conception of an ideal republic, in which order would be maintained only if each individual had only one task.
4 [marginal note] Trades taught to satisfy need, not greed.
5 [marginal note] A uniform dress code.
6 [marginal note] No citizen without a trade.

labor. As a rule, a son is brought up in his father's craft, for which he usually has a natural inclination, but anyone attracted to another sort of work is adopted by a family pursuing it.[1] Parents and officials strive to ensure that such a child joins a serious and honest household. Moreover, those already expert in one craft who want to learn a second may do so; having acquired both, they practice whichever they please unless the city has more need of one than the other.

The chief and almost only function of the Syphogrants is to see that no one sits idle but pursues a craft zealously.[2] No one, however, is wearied like a beast of burden by constant toil from early morning till late at night, a wretchedness worse than slavery. Outside Utopia, that is the usual lot of laborers.[3] Utopians divide the day and night into twenty-four equal hours, assigning only six to labor. People work for three hours before noon, after which they go to dinner. After resting for two hours, they do three more and then go to supper.[4] At about 8 p.m. they go to bed and sleep for eight hours. Each person decides how to pass the leisure hours, so long as he does not fritter them away in sloth and roistering but pursues some interest to which he is inclined. Many devote these breaks to literature and learning.[5] For their custom is to hold daily public lectures in the early morning, and although only those specially chosen to devote themselves to learning have to attend, a great number of men and women from every line of work go to hear whichever lecture appeals to them. They do not blame those many who prefer spending time on their craft rather than on intellectual matters, and in fact commend them as useful citizens. After supper they spend one hour in recreation, in summer in the gardens and in winter in the common halls where they have their meals.[6] There they either practice music or entertain themselves with conversation. They know nothing of throwing the dice and other such stupid and hurtful pursuits.[7] They do play two games not unlike chess—one a battle of numbers in which one number takes another, the other a game in which vices

---

1 [marginal note] Everyone to learn the trade for which his nature fits him.
2 [marginal note] The idle are expelled from society.
3 *Outside ... laborers* In England at that time, laborers worked from sunrise to sunset.
4 [marginal note] Workmen not to be overtasked.
5 [marginal note] The study of letters.
6 [marginal note] Diversion after supper.
7 [marginal note] But now gambling is the sport of kings.

fight a pitched battle with virtues.[1] The game cleverly shows the strife among the vices and their concerted opposition to the virtues. It shows which vices oppose which virtues; by what means they attack openly, and by what contrivances they do so indirectly; by what reinforcement the virtues break the power of the vices and by what arts they frustrate their designs; and, finally, by what means one side gains the victory.[2]

But here, lest you misunderstand, there is one matter to which we should return. Since Utopians spend only six hours working, you might think that some scarcity of goods must follow. But this is far from the case: the time is more than ample to supply a wealth of necessities, even of conveniences. You must bear in mind that a large part of the population in other countries does not work.[3] First, almost no women (half of the population) do so, and where the women are busy, almost as a rule, the men are snoring. Second, there is the great and idle company of secular priests and the so-called "religious" clergy. Add to them the rich, and especially the landowners commonly called gentlemen and noblemen. Now add their retainers—I mean that rabble of good-for-nothing swaggering bullies.[4] Finally, add those beggars who are perfectly able to work but who fake some disease as an excuse for laziness, and you will certainly find that those who produce everything that people need for daily use are fewer by far than you had supposed.[5] Now, of those who do work calculate how few ply essential trades. In a society that makes money the standard of everything, inevitably many crafts are vain and superfluous, serving luxury and extravagance. If the number of those who now work were assigned to only those few crafts supplying the needs and conveniences that Nature demands, there would be such a flood of goods that prices would fall drastically and many would lose their

---

1 *vices fight ... virtues* In More's England the most familiar vices were the seven deadly sins (pride, envy, wrath, sloth, greed, gluttony, and lust) and their opposite virtues (the biblical trio faith, hope, and charity, together with the Aristotelian prudence, temperance, fortitude, and justice); in still pagan Utopia, the virtues are more likely to be those of Aristotle, and their opposing vices the many mentioned by Roman moral philosophers. Moralized chess was found also in Europe. Numbers were on European minds, for the Arabic numerals were still new to many places.
2 [marginal note] Their games are useful too.
3 [marginal note] Kinds of idlers.
4 [marginal note] Noblemen's bodyguards.
5 [marginal note] A very shrewd observation.

jobs. But if all those now busied with unneeded labor, together with all the lazy and idle crowd (each one of whom now consumes as much of the fruits of other men's efforts as any two laborers), were made to do something useful, you would easily see how little time it would take to produce all that is required by necessity, comfort, or even pleasure.

The experience of Utopia makes all this clear. In any city and its immediate neighborhood, exemption from work is granted to no more than five hundred of those men and women whose age and strength makes them fit for toil. The Syphogrants, though released by law from work, take no advantage of this privilege, so that by their example they may inspire others to labor.[1] Others, on the recommendation of priests and by a secret vote of the Syphogrants are granted permanent freedom from labor so that they might devote themselves to study, although anyone who disappoints the hopes placed in him must become a laborer once more. On the other hand, it often happens that someone so industriously devotes his spare hours to learning and makes such progress that he is relieved of manual labor and promoted to the scholarly order. It is out of this group that Utopians choose ambassadors, priests, Tranibors, and finally the governor himself,[2] whom in their ancient tongue was the "Barzanes," but who is now called the "Ademos."[3]

Because the rest of the people are neither idling nor busied with useless occupations, it is easy to reckon what good work can be accomplished in a few hours. In addition to what I have mentioned, there is the further convenience that most of the necessary crafts do not require as much work as they do in other nations.[4] Take, for example, the building or repair of houses. In most places, this requires the constant labor of a great many men simply because what a father builds his extravagant heir lets decay. Consequently, what might have been kept up at small cost must now be rebuilt at great expense. Even if a house has cost one man a large sum, another man is so fastidious that he thinks little of it, lets it crumble, and then builds

---

1 [marginal note]   Not even officials dodge work.
2 [marginal note]   Only the learned hold public office.
3 *Barzanes*   Probably from the Hebrew *bar* (son of) and *Zanos* (of Zeus); *Ademos*   "Peopleless," from the Greek *a* (without) and *demos* (people).
4 [marginal note]   Avoiding expense in building.

another elsewhere at no less cost. But in the Utopians' well-ordered and well-regulated commonwealth, people seldom find new sites for new houses. Not only do they quickly remedy present defects, they also prevent future damages. So with little labor, houses last a long time and masons and carpenters sometimes have scarcely anything to do, although they are told to prepare timber at home and use the time gained to square stone, so that if any work is required they can do it quickly.

As for clothing, see again how little labor is required.[1] While Utopians are at work they dress casually in hide or skins that last for seven years. When they go outdoors they put on a cloak to hide their working clothes; all over the island, this garment has the same natural color. Thus they need much less woolen cloth than is required elsewhere and what they have is less expensive; such cloth is made with less labor, and less of it is consumed. For linen cloth, they care only that it be clean and white; they don't worry about the fineness of thread. So whereas elsewhere one man is not satisfied with four or five woolen gowns of different colors and as many silk coats (and for the more demanding not even ten is enough), in Utopia a man is content with one coat, generally for two years. There is no reason to desire more, for more would not better fortify him against the cold or make him appear better dressed.

With everyone devoted to useful work and satisfied with few goods, sometimes when there is a superabundance of supplies, a great number of citizens are set to fixing roads that are in bad shape. Or, if there is nothing of that kind that needs doing, the officials announce that there will be fewer hours of work. For they do not keep the citizens against their will at unnecessary labor. The constitution of the commonwealth has one objective: that so far as public needs permit, as much time as possible should be taken from serving the body and devoted to the freedom and cultivation of the mind. In that, they believe, consists the happiness of life.

---

1   [marginal note]   Avoiding expense in clothing.

Chapter 5
Their Dealings With One Another

Now I should explain the relations of the citizens one to another, how they treat each other, and how they distribute goods.

Because a city consists of families, the households for the most part consist of those related by blood, although women, when they arrive at maturity and get married, go live in their husbands' houses. Male children and the next generation remain in the family and answer to the oldest parent, unless his mind has become unfit from age, in which case the next oldest is put in his place. Lest any city either be depopulated or grow beyond measure, though, no family of the six thousand that each city (apart from the surrounding district) contains may have fewer than ten or more than sixteen adults.[1] No number can be fixed for underage children. This rule is easily observed by transferring some members of overly large families to those that have too few. If the whole number of citizens surpasses the fixed limit, then they make up any deficient population of other cities. But if the whole island becomes overpopulated they select citizens from each city to go to the mainland nearest them and found a colony wherever the inhabitants have unoccupied and unused land. There they live under their own laws, letting the natives who wish to do so join them. When the two groups do blend, the two peoples easily grow into the same way of life and manners, to the great advantage of both. Using Utopian methods, they make the land sufficient for both groups whereas it had once seemed barely adequate for one. If the natives refuse to live according to Utopian laws, the settlers drive them out of the territory that they have claimed. If such natives resist, they fight them, for they think it a most just cause for war whenever a people does not use its soil but keeps it vacant and even forbid others, whose natural right it is to be nourished by it, to use and possess it. If an accident diminishes the citizenry of any Utopian city so badly that the loss cannot be made up by people from other parts of the island without bringing their cities, too, below their proper strength (this has happened only once in all the ages, when a fierce plague raged), they bring back settlers from the colony. They would rather lose colonies than let any of the island's cities weaken.

---

1 [marginal note]   The number of citizens.

To return to the family life of the citizens: the oldest, as I said, rules the family. Wives serve their husbands, children their parents, and generally the younger minister to their elders.[1] Every city is divided into four quarters. In the middle of each quarter is a market for all kinds of goods. There the products of each family are conveyed and each kind of is put in separate storehouses. From these, any father of a family takes what he and his family require, and without money or any kind of payment he carries it off. Why should anything be refused? All things are plentiful, and there is no fear that anyone will demand more than he needs. Why should he, when he knows he will never lack anything?[2] In all creatures, only fear of want causes greed; only in human beings does pride lead some to think it glorious to excel in displays of excess. This vice can have no place among Utopians.

Next to the marketplaces I have mentioned are provision markets to which are brought, from sites outside the city where running water washes away all disease and filth,[3] vegetables, fruit, and bread, as well as fish and all edible beasts and birds. In those outer areas, slaves clean the animal carcasses, for Utopians do not allow free citizens to accustom themselves to butchering animals, thinking that such a practice erodes mercy, the finest quality of our nature.[4] Nor do they allow inside the city anything dirty or unclean lest the air be tainted by putrefaction and spread disease.

Every street has spacious halls at equal distance from one another and with special names. In these live the Syphogrants, to each of whom are appointed thirty families, fifteen on either side, with whom to share meals. The caterers of each hall meet at a fixed time in the market and get enough food for the appropriate number of people.

Special care is taken of the sick, who are looked after in one of the four public hospitals that are spaced out at the edges of town, a little outside the walls.[5] These are so roomy that they seem like small towns;[6] the purpose is to prevent the sick, however numerous, from being packed close in discomfort, and also to isolate the contagious and thus prevent their passing on their maladies to others. These hos-

---

1 [marginal note] Thus they eliminate crowds of idle servants.

2 [marginal note] The sources of greed.

3 [marginal note] Filth and garbage spread disease in cities.

4 [marginal note] By butchering beasts we learn to slaughter men.

5 [marginal note] Caring for the sick.

6 *These ... towns* England at this time had a number of hospitals, but none on this scale.

pitals are so well furnished and equipped with everything conducive to health, and the expert attending physicians provide such delicate and careful treatment, that although no one is sent there involuntarily there is hardly anybody in the whole city who, when ill, does not prefer to be cared for there rather than at home.

When the hospital caterer has received the food prescribed by the physicians, the rest is equally distributed among the halls according to the number in each, except that special consideration is given to the Governor, the Bishop, the Tranibors, and to ambassadors and foreigners, if any. Foreigners seldom visit, but when they do, they have special housing.

A trumpet blast summons the whole Syphogranty to assemble in these halls at the fixed hours for dinner and supper, except for those who are in hospital or who take their meals at their own houses.[1] No one is forbidden to bring extra food from the market to his house after the halls have been served. Utopians know that this is never done without good reason,[2] for while no one is forbidden to dine at home, no one does so willingly—it is seen as inappropriate. It seems foolish to bother preparing an inferior dinner when a rich and sumptuous one is all ready in a nearby hall. In the hall slaves perform all tasks that demand heavy work and soil the hands. The women, from each family by turns, cook and serve the food and arrange the whole meal.[3] They sit down at three or more tables according to the number of the company, the men with their backs to the wall and the women on the outside, so that if any they feel any sudden sickness or pangs, as often happens during pregnancy, they may easily rise and go see the nurses without disturbing others.

The nurses sit apart with the infants in a special room supplied with a fire, clean water, and cradles, so that when they wish they can lay the infants down or take them by the fire and let them play. Each woman nurses her own child unless prevented by death or disease. When that happens, the wives of the Syphogrants quickly provide a nurse and find no difficulty in doing so.[4] Those who can do the

---

1 [marginal note] Meals in common, mixing all groups.
2 [marginal note] Note how freedom is granted everywhere, lest people act under compulsion.
3 [marginal note] Women prepare the meals.
4 [marginal note] Honor and praise incite people to act properly.

service offer themselves with the greatest readiness, since everyone values this kind of charity and the child sees his nurse as his natural mother. In the nurses' quarters are all the children up to five years old;[1] all the others below the age of marriage either wait on their elders or, if not old and strong enough, stand by in absolute silence. Both groups of children eat what is handed to them from the table and have no other separate mealtimes.

The Syphogrant and his wife sit in the middle of the high table, the place of honor, from which they can view the whole company, their table standing crosswise at the end of the room. Alongside sit two of the elderly, for there are always four at a table. If there is a temple in the Syphogranty, the priest and his wife sit with the Syphogrant and preside.[2] On both sides of them sit the younger and next to them, old men again, and so it is throughout the house that those of the same age sit together, and yet still associate with those of a different age.[3] The reason, they say, is to let the grave and reverend behavior of the senior restrain the junior from mischievous words and gestures, since nothing can be done or said at the table that escapes the notice of older neighbors.

The courses are not served in order from the top place down; rather, old men, seated in specially marked places, are served first, with the best food, and then equal portions go to the rest.[4] But the senior, at their discretion, give a share of their delicacies to their neighbors if there are not enough of these for everyone. Thus due respect is paid to age and yet equality is honored. Every meal starts with some reading conducive to morality but brief enough not to become boring.[5] Next the elders introduce good topics of conversation, not too serious or devoid of wit.[6] But they do not take up the whole dinner with long speeches, for they enjoy hearing the young men too, and indeed, try to draw them out, testing the ability and talent that are revealed in the freedom of conversation. Their dinners are somewhat short, their suppers more prolonged, because the first are followed by labor, the latter by sleep and rest, which they think more effective for whole-

---

1 [marginal note]   Raising the young.
2 [marginal note]   Priest before prince. But now even bishops act as servants to royalty.
3 [marginal note]   Young mixed with old.
4 [marginal note]   Respect for the elderly.
5 [marginal note]   Not even monks do this now.
6 [marginal note]   Table talk.

some digestion.[1] No supper passes without music, nor does any meal lack dessert.[2] They burn spices, and scatter perfumes, and omit nothing that might cheer the company; for they enjoy such things, and regard no pleasure as illicit that does no harm.[3]

Life in the city is communal, but in the country those who live far from others take their meals in their own homes. No family lacks any kind of food, however, for whatever the city-dwellers eat comes from the country.

Chapter 6
Traveling

Those struck with a desire to visit friends in another city or to see the country may easily get leave from their Syphogrants and Tranibors unless there is good reason against it. Right away a party is formed and departs, bearing a letter from the Governor certifying their permission to travel and naming the day of their return. They are given a wagon with a community slave to drive it and to tend to the oxen, but unless they have women with them they leave the carriage behind as a burden and hindrance.

Throughout their journey, although carrying nothing with them, they lack for nothing, being at home everywhere. If they stay longer than a day in any one place, each plies his trade and finds warm hospitality among his brethren of the same craft. Anyone caught outside his territory's limits without a certificate, however, is scorned as a runaway and punished severely; should he rashly repeat the offence he is made a slave. If anyone wants to explore the country around his own city, though, he may do so if he gets his father's leave and his wife's consent. Wherever he goes, however, he is given no food until he completes a morning's worth of work, or so much work as is usually performed between dinner and supper. If he fulfills his responsibility, he may go where he please within the city's territorial limits, for he will be just as useful to it there as if he were in town. So you can see that there is no way of evading work and no pretext for idleness: no wine shop, no ale house, no brothel, no occasion for depravity, no

---

1 [marginal note] Modern doctors think ill of this practice.
2 [marginal note] Music at mealtimes.
3 [marginal note] Innocent pleasures are not to be rejected.

lurking holes, no secret meetings.[1] Everything is open to everyone, and everyone is bound either to do the usual work or to take lawful and not indecent recreation.

A people following such customs inevitably produce an ample store of everything. And because it is distributed evenly to everyone, nobody is forced into poverty or beggary.[2] The Senate of Amaurote, to which as I have said every city annually sends three members, determines what goods abound in one place or are lacking in another, then fills the shortage in one place with the overflow from another. There is no payment, no taking of anything from those to whom is given, and those who have given freely from their surplus to one city can in turn get what they need from another, thus the whole island is like a single family.[3]

When the Utopians have laid up enough for themselves (figuring that it should last for two years in case of crop failure), then they export to other countries a great deal of grain, honey, wool, linen, wood, scarlet and purple dye, fleeces, wax, tallow,[4] leather, and surplus livestock. They give one-seventh of these goods to the poor of that region and sell the rest at a moderate price.[5] By this exchange they import not only whatever they lack themselves—and practically everything is found in Utopia except iron—but also a great deal of silver and gold. The custom has stood so long that now they have everywhere plenty of these things—more than one would believe—so they care little whether they are paid immediately or later, and usually have much owed to them.

Whenever they are not paid at once, they do not trust the credit of individuals but rather that of a city, as a rule requiring signed promises.[6] When the day for payment arrives, the city collects the money owed by private debtors, puts it into the treasury, and enjoys the use of it until the Utopians claim payment.[7] But for the most part they do not demand repayment, thinking it unfair to take away something useful to others when they do not require it themselves. If other

---

1 [marginal note] O sacred society, worthy of imitation, especially by Christians!
2 [marginal note] Equality for all results in enough for each.
3 [marginal note] The commonwealth is nothing but a kind of extended family.
4 *tallow* Animal fat used in soap and candle production.
5 [marginal note] Utopian business dealings.
6 [marginal note] Never do they fail to be mindful of the community.
7 [marginal note] How money can be useful.

people do need it, however, they call in their debts so as to make a new loan. They do the same whenever a war impends, for war is the only reason for keeping treasure at home and thus available for use in extreme peril or a sudden emergency.[1] They primarily use such treasure to pay extravagant sums to foreign mercenaries, whom they would rather hazard than their own citizens, knowing that with such huge cash reserves even their enemies might be purchased and set to fight one another by deceit or open warfare. For this reason they keep a vast treasure, but not *as* treasure. I almost blush to say how they keep it, lest I be disbelieved. Had I not been there and witnessed it, I would have difficulty crediting it myself,[2] for in general the more alien something is to the manners and ways of those who hear, the farther it is from what they can believe. An impartial judge, though, knowing that their other customs are so unlike our own, will not be surprised that their treatment of gold and silver suits their way of life, not ours. And, again, they do not use money themselves but keep it for emergencies that may or may not come.

In the meantime, gold and silver, of which money is made, are treated so that no one values them more than they merit by their nature. Anyone can see that gold and silver are less useful than iron, for iron is as vital to human life, by Heaven, as are fire and water. Nature gave gold and silver no utility—it is only our folly that makes them seem precious.[3] Rather, like a kind and indulgent parent, she exposed to our sight all that is best, such as air, water, and earth itself, and has hidden away as far as possible all vain and unprofitable things.

Now if in Utopia these metals were kept locked up in a tower, it might be suspected—for such is the foolish imagination of the common people—that the Governor and the Council were craftily deceiving the public and profiting at its expense. Moreover, Utopians know that if they turned the metal into drinking cups or other objects of skilful handiwork, then, if they needed to melt them down again so as to hire soldiers, people would be unwilling to lose what they had begun to treasure. To avoid these dangers, they have devised a method that fits their own culture but would seem incredible to anyone who

---

1   [marginal note]   Better to avoid war by bribery or guile than to wage it with great bloodshed.
2   [marginal note]   O crafty fellow!
3   [marginal note]   As far as utility goes, gold is inferior to iron.

had not been there, so much do we value gold and so careful are we to hoard it. They themselves eat and drink from earthenware and glass of fine workmanship if of little value. But to make chamberpots and other indecent containers for both public halls and private houses they use gold and silver.[1] They use the same metals for their slaves' chains, and they make those who are to be publicly shamed for some offence wear gold earrings, finger rings, necklaces, and coronets. Thus by every means in their power they turn gold and silver into marks of disgrace.[2] Some nations take the loss of these same metals harder than they would a disemboweling, but in Utopia, if all gold and silver were taken in a single crisis, no one would feel that he had lost as much as a penny.

Utopians do gather pearls by the seashore, and value certain stones such as diamonds and garnets, but they do not go searching for them. When they chance upon them, they polish them up and give them to children, who when they are little take delight and pride in such ornaments.[3] After they grow up, however, and see that only children value these toys, they lay them aside, not thanks to orders from their parents but through their own sense of adult self-respect, just as our young, when they grow up, lay aside their marbles, rattles, and dolls.

Different customs, different attitudes.[4] This struck me forcibly during a visit by the Anemolian[5] ambassadors, who came to Amaurote during my stay there. In their honor, the city had assembled ahead of time three representatives of each city in the island. Now, the ambassadors of nearby nations, who had already visited Utopia and knew its customs, were well aware that Utopians have no respect for costly clothes, look with contempt on silk, and regard gold as a badge of disgrace, so they usually arrived in the simplest possible dress. But the Anemolians lived farther off and had had fewer dealings with Utopians. Knowing that in Utopia all dressed alike and with equal simplicity, they had assumed that Utopians must not have what they do not wear, and so, being more proud than wise, they had planned to play the gods by the fineness of their clothing and thus dazzle the eyes of the poor natives. And so the three ambassadors made a grand

---

1 [marginal note] O magnificent scorn for gold!
2 [marginal note] Gold the mark of infamy.
3 [marginal note] Gems the playthings of children.
4 [marginal note] A neat tale.
5 *Anemolian* Windy; from the Greek *anemolios*.

entry with an entourage of a hundred followers, all in multicolored clothes, mostly of silk. The ambassadors themselves, who were noblemen at home, were splendid in cloth of gold, with big chains of gold and gold earrings, with gold rings on their fingers, and with strings of pearls and precious stones upon their caps—in short, decked out with the very things that in Utopia are used to punish slaves, stigmatize evildoers, or amuse children. And so it was a sight to see how they strutted when they compared their grand clothing with the dress of the Utopians, who had poured into the streets to see them pass. It was no less amusing to notice how mistaken they were in their overconfidence and how far from winning the admiration they had expected. For the Utopians, with the exception of those very few who had visited other countries, found all this gaudy show disgraceful. So they bowed to the lowest of the party but ignored the ambassadors and paid them no deference, thinking them slaves because of their gold. Indeed, you might have seen those children who had discarded pearls and precious stones nudge their mothers at the sight of such things on the caps of the ambassadors and say, "Look at that big idiot, Mother, still wearing pearls and gems like a kid."[1] The mothers in all seriousness would answer, "Hush, son, I think he's one of the ambassadors' jesters." Others called the gold chains useless: so slender that a slave could easily break them, or so loose that he could slip them off and escape. For a couple of days the ambassadors watched as their stupendous show of gold was slighted—indeed, disregarded to the same degree that they had hoped for honor. Then they observed that there was more gold and silver in the chains and fetters of a single runaway slave than in all of their finery put together. Crestfallen and ashamed, all the more so as they became more familiar with the Utopians and their ways, they put away all the finery with which they had made themselves so conspicuous.

The Utopians wonder how any mortal can take pleasure in the uncertain sparkle of a tiny gem or shiny pebble stone when he can look at a star or at the sun itself.[2] They wonder how anyone can be lunatic enough to think himself grander than others because he wears wool of a thinner thread: however finely spun it is, a sheep once wore it and the sheep is still just a sheep. They wonder, too, that gold, in

---

1   [marginal note]   The rascal!
2   [marginal note]   "Weak" because the gems are false, or the glitter is feeble and scanty.

its own nature so useless, is now everywhere valued so highly that humanity itself, by whom and for whose use it got its value, is priced far below gold. They cannot comprehend that a leaden-head who has no more wit than a post and is no less wicked than foolish can keep in bondage many wise and good men merely because he has a great heap of gold coins.[1] Yet if this dolt, by chance or legal chicanery, loses that gold to the lowest rascal of the household (for the law can reverse the high and low as arbitrarily as can fortune), he will surely become a slave of his former servant, as if he had been a mere appendage or adjunct of the money. Much more are they aghast at the madness of those who almost worship the rich even though neither owing them anything nor being in any fashion beholden to them and impressed only by their wealth.[2] This especially surprises the Utopians, for they know that these men are so mean and miserly that probably of all that pile of cash, so long as the rich men live, not a penny will ever come their way. These and similar opinions they have derived partly from their upbringing in a commonwealth with institutions free from such folly and partly from reading books.

Only a few in each city are relieved from other work so as to devote themselves exclusively to study: those who have shown from childhood talent, high intelligence, and a fine disposition. Nevertheless, all children are trained in good letters, and many people, men and women alike, throughout their lives spend those hours that I said were free from manual labor on learning. They study the various branches of knowledge in their own language, for it is rich in vocabulary, pleasing to the ear, and well adapted for expressing thought.[3] Much of that part of the world has the same language, though sometimes in a variety of corrupted forms.

Philosophers whose names are famous to us were unknown to Utopians before our arrival, yet in music, dialectic, arithmetic and geometry they have made almost the same discoveries as our forebears.[4] Just as they equal the ancients in almost all respects, however, so they fall far short of our inventive modern logicians,[5] for they have

---

1 [marginal note]   How true and how apt!
2 [marginal note]   How much wiser are the Utopians than the common sort of Christians.
3 [marginal note]   Training and studies of the Utopians.
4 [marginal note]   Music, dialectic, and mathematics.
5 [marginal note]   The passage seems a bit satiric.

not discovered a single one of those ingeniously derived rules about restrictions, amplifications, and suppositions that our children learn in the *Parva Logicalia*.[1] They are so far from being able to find out second intentions,[2] that not one of them was able to catch sight of "Humanity" in the abstract, even after we pointed at him with our fingers, though "Humanity" is, as you know, a Colossus greater than any giant. But they are most expert in the paths of the stars and the movements of the celestial bodies.[3] Furthermore, they have cleverly devised instruments of different shapes by which they have most exactly understood the movements and positions of the sun and moon and the other stars they see in the sky. But of the agreements and discords of the planets, and of all deceitful divination by the stars, they do not even dream.[4] They forecast rain, wind and changes in the weather by certain signs that they have learned to recognize after long practice. As for the causes of all these things, however, or on the flow of the sea and its saltiness, or in sum on the origin and nature of the heavens and the universe, they sometimes agree with our ancient natural philosophers or, like our own experts, sometimes introduce new theories that disagree with all earlier ones—nor do they always agree with each other.[5]

As for moral philosophy, they discuss the same topics that we do.[6] They inquire into the goods of the soul, goods of the body, and external goods.[7] They also wonder whether the name of "good" may be rightly applied to all three or belongs only to the endowments of the soul.[8] They discuss virtue and pleasure, but chiefly they discuss in what thing—or things—happiness consists.[9] In this matter

---

1   *Parva Logicalia*   Latin: Little Logical Works. Texts with this or similar titles were made by Medieval Nominalist philosophers, for whom Renaissance humanists had little liking, although they still studied them. Hence More's allusion to "good letters"—to some extent what we call "literature" and a contrast to the late medieval stress on logic.

2   *second intentions*   "First intentions" are the direct apprehensions of material objects; "second intentions" are abstract conceptions derived from generalizations upon first intentions.

3   [marginal note]   The study of the stars.

4   [marginal note]   Yet these astrologers are revered by Christians to this very day.

5   [marginal note]   Physics the most uncertain study of all.

6   [marginal note]   Ethics.

7   [marginal note]   Higher and lower goods.

8   *They also wonder ... soul*   This first position is that of the Aristotelians; the second is held by the Stoics.

9   [marginal note]   Supreme goods.

they seem to lean more than they should to the school that defends pleasure, since they believe it to be the whole or at least chief cause of human happiness.[1] More astonishing, they try to defend this soft philosophy with principles taken from their religion, which is grave and strict, even stern and rigid.[2] They never discuss happiness without joining some principles derived from religion to reasoning drawn from philosophy.[3] Without these principles, they think, reason is too weak and insufficient to investigate true happiness.

These principles are that the soul is immortal, that thanks to God's goodness it is born to be happy, and that after this life our virtues and good deeds are rewarded and our crimes punished.[4] Although these principles are matters of faith, Utopians think that reason leads us to believe and acknowledge them.[5] If they were set aside, they hasten to add, nobody would be so stupid as not to seek pleasure by means fair or foul. He should take care only to stop a lesser pleasure from interfering with a greater one, or to avoid pleasure that leads to pain.[6] For to seek a hard and painful virtue, and not only drive away all enjoyment but voluntarily to suffer pain that without later profit—for what profit can there be if after death you get nothing for having spent your whole life unpleasantly, even wretchedly?—this they hold to be utter nonsense. But as it is, the Utopians think happiness rests not in *all* kinds of pleasure, but rather in those that are good and honorable. To these, as to the supreme good, our nature is drawn by virtue itself (to which alone the opposite school of philosophy attributes happiness).[7]

Utopians define virtue as living according to nature, since God created us to that end.[8] Whoever obeys the dictates of reason in desiring one thing and avoiding another, they say, follows the guidance of

---

1   *In this ... happiness*   This reflects an Epicurean position that sensuous pleasures were the only happiness available in the material world.

2   [marginal note]   The Utopians consider honest pleasure the measure of happiness.

3   [marginal note]   First principles of philosophy to be sought in religion.

4   [marginal note]   Utopian theology.

5   [marginal note]   The immortality of the soul, on which nowadays no small number even of Christians have their doubts.

6   [marginal note]   Not every pleasure is desirable, neither is pain to be sought, except for the sake of virtue.

7   *school ... happiness*   This is the Stoic view, which emphasizes morality, virtue, and duty over material pleasures.

8   [marginal note]   This is like Stoic doctrine.

nature. Reason, first of all, inspires us to love and venerate the Divine Majesty who gave us our lives and our capacity for happiness. Second, reason urges and admonishes us to lead lives as free from care and as full of joy as possible, and, because of our natural fellowship, to help others do likewise. No one was ever such a solemn and strict follower of virtue and hater of pleasure that however hard the labor, wakefulness, and discomfort he urged on you he would not also tell you to do your best to relieve the poverty and discomfort of others. He would tell you to think it praiseworthy, in the name of humanity, for one person to provide for another's health and comfort. Now, if it is especially humane (and this is the virtue most peculiar to humankind) to relieve the misery of others, to take away sorrow from their lives, and to restore enjoyment and pleasure, why should not nature urge us to do the same for ourselves? For if a joyous and pleasurable life is evil, then you should not only not help anyone experience joy and pleasure, you should even try to take these away from everyone else on the grounds that they are harmful and deadly.[1] On the other hand, if you feel bound to praise such a life as good for them, then you should do the same for yourself, to whom you should show no less favor than to others. When nature bids you to be good to others, she does not command you to be cruel and merciless to yourself. Nature herself, the Utopians say, calls us to a merry life, so that, in sum, pleasure is the end of all activity, and to live according to her prescriptions is virtue. But even though Nature calls us all to help each other to a merrier life (for she regards no one as raised so far above the common human lot as to be the sole object of her care), she surely bids you take constant care not to favor yourself so much that you put others at a disadvantage.

Utopians think not only that all bargains between individuals should be observed, but also that the common laws should be obeyed by everyone. Provided that they have been proclaimed by a just ruler and ratified by common consent, such laws provide just rules for the fair distribution of material goods, or, in other words, the means of pleasure.[2] So long as these laws are not broken, it is wisdom to look

---

1 [marginal note]   But now some people cultivate pain as if it were the essence of religion, rather than incidental to performance of a pious duty or the result of natural necessity— and thus to be borne, not pursued.

2 [marginal note]   Contracts and laws.

after your own interests and your duty to take care of the public interest as well. To deprive others of their pleasure so as to secure your own is injustice, while to take away something from yourself to give to others is a duty of humanity and kindness, which never takes away as much as it gives back. First, you are for the most part eventually compensated by a return of benefits. Second, the consciousness of having done a good deed is a benefit in itself. And receiving the love and goodwill of those whom you have benefited gives your mind a greater pleasure than the bodily pleasure you have given up.[1] Finally—this is brought home to those of a religious bent—in return for a brief and small pleasure God repays you with great and endless joy. So the Utopians, having carefully considered and weighed the matter, believe that all our actions and even our virtues have pleasure as their final purpose.

By pleasure they understand every activity or state of body or mind in which a person delights under the guidance of nature.[2] They are right to specify a person's *natural* inclinations.[3] The senses and right reason aim at whatever is naturally pleasant—that is, at whatever is not achieved by wrong-doing, does not involve the loss of something more pleasant, and is not followed by pain. But there are some disagreeable things that mortals unnaturally imagine by a foolish consensus to be agreeable (as though mortals could change the nature of things as easily as they do their names).[4] Not only do these things not cause any happiness, they seriously hinder it, for once rooted in the mind they possess it with a false idea of pleasure, leaving no room for true and natural delights. There are many things which by nature are not sweet—indeed, are usually very bitter—yet which through the perversity of our evil desires we regard as the greatest pleasures and even count among those things that make life most worth living. Among those who follow false pleasure the Utopians include the people I mentioned who think themselves better because

---

1 [marginal note]   Mutual assistance.
2 [marginal note]   What is pleasure?
3 *By pleasure ... inclinations*   The following discussion reflects both Plato's and Aristotle's praise of physical and mental pleasures and their distinctions between true pleasures (those "pleasant by nature") and false ones. See Plato's *Philebus* and Aristotle's *Nicomachean Ethics*. Many of the false pleasures listed here are discussed in More's friend Erasmus's *The Praise of Folly* (1511).
4 [marginal note]   False pleasures.

they wear better clothes.[1] In this one thing such people make two mistakes, for they are just as deceived in thinking their clothes better as in thinking themselves better. If you consider clothing's use, why is fine-spun wool superior to thicker? And yet snobs think not only that the thread is better but also that some extra value thereby attaches to themselves. Dressed in finer threads, they demand a level of respect that they would never hope for if dressed in shabbier clothing. If passed by without visible respect, they get indignant.

And does it not show the same folly to think so much of empty and unprofitable honors?[2] What true and natural pleasure can the bared head or bent knees of another give you? Will this cure the pain in your own knees or relieve the madness in your own head? In this fantasized view of pleasure, men who imagine themselves noble show a strange lunacy, pride themselves on it, and applaud themselves because it has been their fortune to be born of a long succession of rich ancestors (for that is now the only nobility), rich especially in land.[3] But they think themselves not a whit less noble even if their ancestors have not left them an acre, or if they themselves have used up their inheritance through extravagant living.

The Utopians also see as chasing a false pleasure those who dote on jewels and gems, thinking themselves gods if they acquire a fine specimen.[4] They especially ridicule those who most value the most fashionable stones—for the same kinds are not always and everywhere the most highly prized.[5] Such people will not buy gems unless they can see them out of their gold settings, and even then they make the seller swear and offer some security that it is a genuine jewel, a true gem, so anxious are they lest a fake deceive their eyes. But why should a counterfeit stone give less pleasure to the eye if the eye cannot tell it from a true one? Both should be of equal value to you, even as they would be to a blind man.

What can be said of people who keep a surplus of wealth for no other use than to look at? Do they feel any real pleasure, or are they not in fact cheated by an unreal one? And what of people who have

---

1 [marginal note] Mistaken pride in fancy dress.
2 [marginal note] Foolish titles.
3 [marginal note] Empty nobility.
4 [marginal note] The silliest pleasures of all: gemstones.
5 [marginal note] Popular opinion gives gemstones their value or takes it away.

the opposite folly and hide away gold that they will never use and may never see again? In their fear of losing it, they lose it indeed—for what else is it to put it back in the ground and thus deprive themselves (and all others) of its use? And still they exult over their hidden treasure as though quite free of all anxiety. Yet suppose someone were to take it, and the miser then were to die ten years later knowing nothing of the theft. During all those ten years, what would it matter to him whether it was stolen or safe? In either case it would have been of equally little use to him.[1]

Also among those who indulge in senseless delights Utopians number those who turn to gambling, and to hunting and hawking. What true pleasure can there be, they ask, in casting dice into a box?[2] To do it so often, even if there is some pleasure in it, must eventually lead to boredom. Or what true pleasure can there be (and not disgust) in hearing the barking and howling of dogs?[3] How is it more pleasurable if a dog chases a hare than if a dog runs after a dog? The same thing happens in either case. Each has fast running, if that's what you like. Only if you are drawn by the hope of slaughter and the sight of a creature being torn apart in front of you will the former give you more pleasure than the latter. Rather, you should feel pity when you see a poor, weak, timid, and innocent hare rent in pieces by a strong, fierce, and cruel dog. That is why the Utopians have handed over the whole business of hunting, a job unworthy of free citizens, to the butchers (as I said before, they make their slaves butchers).[4] They regard hunting as the most ignoble part of the butcher's craft, and the other parts of his job as more useful and honorable. The butcher does much good and kills animals from necessity, whereas the hunter seeks nothing but pleasure from killing and mangling some poor creature. Utopians think a hunter's desire to see bloodshed either arises from a cruel disposition or creates one as the effect of constant practice in savage pleasure.

Although these and innumerable related pursuits count as pleasures to the common crowd, Utopians hold that they have absolutely nothing to do with real pleasure, since there is nothing *naturally* agreeable in them. That they commonly inspire a feeling of enjoyment (which

---

1 [marginal note] A strange fancy, and much to the point.
2 [marginal note] Dicing.
3 [marginal note] Hunting.
4 [marginal note] Yet today this is the chosen art of our court-divinities.

seems to be the function of pleasure) does not alter this opinion, for the enjoyment does not arise from the nature of the thing but from a perverse habit that leads people to take what is really bitter to be sweet, just as pregnant women with a distorted taste think pitch and tallow sweeter than honey.[1] And yet no person's judgment, however depraved by disease or habit, could change the true nature of pleasure any more than it could change the nature of other things.

The Utopians divide pleasures that they consider genuine into various classes, some belonging to the soul and others to the body.[2] To the soul they ascribe intelligence and the delight that comes from contemplating the truth; to these they add the pleasant recollection of a well-spent life and the confident hope of happiness to come. Bodily pleasure they divide into two categories.[3] The first is that which fills the senses with a perceptible sweetness. This may come by the renewing of those parts that have been emptied by our natural exertion and are restored by food and drink. Sometimes this agreeable sensation comes when some excess is relieved from the overloaded body, as when we move our bowels, engage in the procreative act, or relieve an itch by rubbing or scratching. But sometimes pleasure comes neither from restoring what our bodies lack nor from removing what causes discomfort, for there is a pleasure that tickles and moves us with a secret but remarkable force and attracts the senses: the pleasure engendered by music.

The second category of bodily pleasure, they say, comes from a calm and harmonious state of the body—in a word, health, uninterrupted by any disorder. This is itself delightful, even when not activated by any pleasure applied from without. Although it is less obvious and less perceptible to the senses than the coarser delights of eating and drinking, nonetheless good health is held by many to be the greatest of pleasures. Almost all Utopians so regard it, and it is practically the basis and foundation of all other pleasures, because it alone can make life peaceful and desirable; without it there is no room for any enjoyment.[4] Being without pain but also without health they consider mere dullness, not pleasure.

---

1 [marginal note] Morbid tastes of pregnant women.
2 [marginal note] Varieties of true pleasure.
3 [marginal note] Bodily pleasures.
4 [marginal note] To enjoy anything, one should be in good health.

Utopians long ago rejected the position of those who hold that a state of tranquil and stable health (for this question, too, they have actively discussed) is not to be counted as a pleasure on the grounds that its presence cannot be felt except in contrast with its opposite.[1] Utopians now almost all agree that health is above all things conducive to pleasure. For in disease there is pain, which is pleasure's bitter enemy, just as disease is the enemy of health. So why should we not take pleasure in the complacency of health? Utopians think that it makes no difference whether you call disease pain or pain disease. Both come to the same thing. For if you believe that health is either a pleasure itself or the necessary cause of pleasure, as fire is of heat, in both cases it follows that those in good health cannot be without pleasure. Besides, they say, when we eat, what is that but health fighting against hunger with the aid of food when it was fading? While the body gradually regains strength, the process itself supplies the pleasure by which we are restored. Shall health, which delights in the struggle, not rejoice when it has gained the victory? And, when at last health has successfully found its old strength, which was its sole aim all along, shall it then become insensible and not recognize nor embrace its own good? It is quite false to say that the senses cannot perceive health, the Utopians think, for who when awake does not *feel* that he is in health (unless he is not)? Who is so insensible or lethargic that he does not confess health to be pleasurable and delightful? And what is delight except pleasure under another name?

Above all, Utopians value the pleasures of the mind (they hold them to be the founts and heads of all), and of these the most important arise from the exercise of virtues and the consciousness of a good life.[2] Of all the bodily pleasures, they give the first place to health. Other delights—eating and drinking, and anything that gives the same kind of enjoyment—they also think desirable, but only for the sake of health. For such things are not pleasurable in themselves but only insofar as they resist the secret assaults of disease. And just as a wise man should rather try to prevent disease than seek a remedy for it, so it would be better to have this kind of pleasure than to be

---

1   *Utopians ... opposite*   The position is discussed in Plato's *Republic* 9.583 C-E.
2   *Above all ... life*   See Cicero, *On Old Age* 3.4: "The most suitable defenses of old age are the principles and practice of the virtues, which, if cultivated in every period of life, bring forth wonderful fruits at the close of a long and busy career."

eased of pain. If a man thinks that happiness consists in this kind of pleasure, he must admit that the greatest happiness would be to spend his life in perpetual hunger, thirst, itching, eating, drinking, scratching and rubbing. What could be more disgusting or pathetic? These pleasures must be the lowest of all because they are the least pure, never occurring unless joined with their respective pain.[1] Thus to the pleasure of eating is joined hunger (and on no fair terms: the pain is the stronger and lasts longer, for it comes into being before the pleasure and does not end until the pleasure dies with it.) Such pleasures should not be highly valued except in so far as they are necessary. Yet Utopians enjoy even these, gratefully acknowledging the kindness of Mother Nature, who with enticing sweetness coaxes her offspring into doing what by necessity they must constantly perform. In what discomfort would we live if, like the sicknesses that less frequently assail us, these daily diseases of hunger and thirst could be cured only by bitter medications?

Utopians value beauty, strength and nimbleness as special and pleasant gifts of nature. They also prize even those pleasures that enter by the ears, eyes and nose, pleasures that nature designed to be peculiarly characteristic of our species—for no other kind of living creature takes in the fairness and form of the universe, is affected by the pleasantness of smell (except in connection with food), or distinguishes concordant and discordant musical intervals. But in all these matters Utopians make this limitation: the lesser pleasure must not interfere with the greater, and pleasure must not produce pain. They think the latter inevitable if the pleasure in question is base. But to disdain physical beauty, to waste the body and turn agility into sluggishness, to starve oneself to death, to neglect health and all other favors of Mother Nature—to do any of these things for any reason other than the public good and a greater reward from God they consider extreme madness. It is a delusional pleasure to afflict oneself when this doesn't serve anyone, and self-torment does nothing to alleviate future sufferings that may never come. It is above all an offense to nature to reject her benefits so that one might owe her nothing.

This is their understanding of virtue and pleasure, and they believe that human reason can find nothing truer unless some Heaven-sent

---

1 *These pleasures ... pain*   See Plato, *Gorgias* 494 C.

religion inspires them with something holier.[1] Whether in this they are right or wrong, time does not permit us to examine now, and in any case I have undertaken only to describe their principles, not to defend them, yet of this I am sure: whatever you think of their views, there is nowhere in the world a more excellent people nor a happier commonwealth.[2]

Utopians are active and nimble of body, and stronger than you would expect from their generally short although not minuscule stature. And though their soil is not very fertile nor is their climate very wholesome, they protect themselves by living temperately and repair the defects of the land by hard work. Thus nowhere in the world is there a better supply of grain and cattle, nor a people more vigorous of body and less subject to disease. And so you may behold in Utopia not only farming that improves poor soil by intelligence and industry, but also a whole forest uprooted in one place by human labor and replanted in another. In this they were thinking not so much of abundance as of transport, so that they might have wood closer to the sea, rivers, or the cities themselves. It takes less work to convey grain a long distance by land than it does timber.

The people are in general easy-going, good tempered, skillful with their hands, and fond of leisure but doing their share of manual labor when occasion requires (at other times they are not fond of it). In their devotion to mental study they are unwearied. When they heard from us about Greek learning and letters (except for historians and poets, there was not much in Latin we thought they would like), they were very keen to have us teach them the language and instruct them in the literature.[3] We therefore began to give them lessons, at first more to avoid seeming reluctant to take the trouble than with expectation of success. But soon their progress and diligence showed that our efforts would not be in vain.[4] They began so easily to imitate the shapes of the letters, so readily to pronounce the words, so quickly to learn by heart, and so faithfully to reproduce what they learned, that it would have seemed a miracle, except that we knew most of them signed on not by choice but by an order of the senate, selected

---

1 [marginal note] Note this and note it well.
2 [marginal note] The happiness of the Utopians, and a description of them.
3 [marginal note] The usefulness of the Greek tongue.
4 [marginal note] Their wonderful aptitude for learning.

from among the scholars of exceptional talent and advanced years.[1] In less than three years they were perfect in the language and able to read good authors without difficulty except when the text was faulty. I imagine that they grasped Greek literature all the more easily because it is so allied to their own. Indeed, I suspect that their race is derived from the Greek, because their language, which in other respects resembles Persian, retains some traces of Greek in the names of their cities and officers.

When I was about to set out on my fourth voyage to Utopia, instead of putting on board goods to sell, I took a fairly large bundle of books, having decided not to leave any time soon, and perhaps not at all. I have given them most of Plato, almost all of Aristotle, and Theophrastus[2] on plants. This last, I regret to say got damaged during the voyage when someone left it lying around and an ape who picked it up to play with carelessly tore out several pages from different parts of the book. Of grammarians they have only Lascaris, for I did not take Gaza with me, and no lexicographer but Hesychius and Dioscorides.[3] They are very fond of Plutarch's works and delight in Lucian's pleasantry and wit.[4] Of the poets they have Aristophanes, Homer, Euripides, and Sophocles in the small Aldine editions;[5] of historians they have Thucydides, Herodotus and also Herodian.[6] As for medicine, my companion Tricius Apinatus had brought along some small treatises of Hippocrates and the *Microtechne* of Galen,

---

1 [marginal note]   But now clods and dullards are taught letters, while the best minds are corrupted by pleasures.

2 *Theophrastus*   Student of Aristotle (d. 287 BCE), whose works on botany were still current during More's time.

3 *Lascaris*   Constantine Lascaris (1434–1501), who wrote the first "modern" Greek grammar; *Gaza*   Theodore of Gaza (d. 1478), a translator of Aristotle who also published a Greek grammar; *Hesychius*   Hesychius of Alexandria (c. fifth century CE), noted for his Greek dictionary; *Dioscorides*   Greek physician of the first century who wrote *De Materia Medica*, the first systematic pharmacological text outlining descriptions and uses for plants and medications.

4 *Plutarch*   Greek biographer (c. 45–125 CE); *Lucian*   Greek rhetorician and satirist (c. 120–180 CE).

5 *Aristophanes*   Greek comedy writer (c. 448–380 BCE); *Euripides*   Greek tragedian (c. 480–406 BCE); *Sophocles*   Greek tragedian (c. 495–406 BCE); *Aldine editions*   Editions published by Aldus Manutius (1449–1515), noted Italian printer.

6 *Thucydides*   Greek historian (c. 471–400 BCE) who wrote *The History of the Peloponnesian War*; *Herodotus*   Herodotus of Halicarnassus (c. fifth century BCE), author of *The Histories*; *Herodian*   Roman historian (c. 170–240 CE) noted for his *History of the Empire*.

which they valued highly,[1] for though there is scarcely any nation that needs medicine less, nowhere is it held in greater honor. For them, medical knowledge is one of the finest and most useful parts of philosophy.[2] When they practice this philosophy and search out the hidden secrets of nature, they not only enjoy it but also believe that they win the approval of the Author and Maker of all things.[3] They think that He, like all artificers, set forth the visible mechanism of the world as a spectacle for human beings, whom alone He made capable of appreciating such wonder. He therefore prefers a careful and diligent beholder and admirer of His work to one who like a brute beast passes by so great and marvelous a spectacle ignorant and unimpressed.

The Utopian mind, then, being trained in all learning, is exceedingly successful in the invention of arts that bring pleasure and convenience. Two of these, however, they owe to us: printing and the manufacture of paper. Not entirely to us, for when we showed them our Aldine editions and talked about (since none of us was an expert, I cannot say *explained*) the material of which paper is made and the art of printing, they promptly and accurately guessed how it was done. Though they had earlier written only on skins, bark and papyrus,[4] they now attempted to manufacture paper and print books. Their first attempts were not very successful, but through trial and error they soon mastered both, so that if they had the texts of Greek writers, they would have no lack of books. At present they have nothing more than I have mentioned, but what they have, they now have in many thousands of printed copies.

Whoever visits their country is gladly received if knowledgeable about many nations, gifted in intellect, or experienced in wide travel, for they delight in hearing what is going on in every country, which is why we were so welcome. But few merchants come there. What could they bring to trade except the same iron, or gold and silver that they would rather take back home? And as for what Utopia exports Uto-

---

1   *Tricius Apinatus*   Fictitious character; *Hippocrates*   Greek physician (c. 460–377 BCE); *Microtechne … Galen*   Treatise by Roman physician (c. 131–201 CE).

2   [marginal note]   Medicine most useful of all studies.

3   [marginal note]   Contemplation of nature.

4   *skins … papyrus*   Writing materials made of animal skins (predominantly calf and sheep and called vellum), the outer portion of trees, and fibers of the papyrus (an Egyptian rush plant), respectively.

pians think it wiser to transport it themselves than to let others come and fetch it, so that by traveling they might acquire more information about foreign nations while also honing their navigational skills.

Chapter 7
Slavery

They do not enslave prisoners of war except those they take themselves.[1] Nor do they force the children of slaves into bondage, nor slaves whom they could get in other countries. Their slaves are either made such in their own country for heinous crimes or have been condemned to death elsewhere for some offence; most of their slaves are of this latter kind. Utopians bring away many such people from other lands, sometimes buying them cheaply or, often, just asking for them and getting them for nothing. Both sorts of slaves, foreigners and Utopians, are kept at work and in chains, but Utopians treat their own countrymen more harshly. These they regard as more deserving of exemplary punishment because despite their good education in virtuous living they could not restrain themselves from crime. There is also another sort of slave: poor laborers in other countries who voluntarily exchange their drudgery for slavery in Utopia. Except for having somewhat more work assigned to them, these are treated almost as well as are citizens. If anyone of this class of slave wishes to leave, which seldom happens, he is not detained against his will or sent away empty handed.

The sick, as I said, are very lovingly cared for; nothing is left undone that might restore them to health, whether medicine or diet.[2] Those suffering from incurable disease they console by sitting and conversing with them and by applying all possible alleviations. But if the disease brings unceasingly pain and trauma, the priests and the magistrates urge the sufferer, now unfit for all the duties of life and become a living burden to himself as well as a distress to others, to cease fostering disease and plague and be willing to die, now that living is an anguish, and so liberate himself from a life as bitter as imprisonment or torture—or let others liberate him.[3] In this the

---

1   [marginal note]   The wonderful fairness of these people.
2   [marginal note]   The sick.
3   [marginal note]   Deliberate death.

sufferer will act wisely, since death will put an end not to enjoyment but to torment, and since in so doing he will be obeying the counsels of the priests, interpreters of God's will, his death would be a pious and devout act.

Those convinced by these arguments either starve themselves to death or, being put to sleep, are released without the sensation of dying. But they do not do away with anyone against his will; nor in such a case do they at all relax their care. They think a death sanctioned by authority is honorable but that anyone who kills himself without the consent of priests and Council is unworthy of fire or earth; without a proper burial, his disgraced body is tossed into a marsh.

Women may not marry before eighteen, men not until they are four years older.[1] Anyone convicted of premarital intercourse is punished severely; such people are forbidden to marry altogether unless pardoned by the governor. The father and mother in whose house such an offence was committed incur great disgrace for having been neglectful. Utopians made this severe law because they foresaw that few would join in conjugal love, spend all of life with one companion, and bear the vexations and troubles that are incident to marriage unless all were restrained from sexual promiscuity.

In choosing mates they seriously and strictly follow a custom that we thought idiotic and utterly ridiculous.[2] The woman, whether maiden or widow, is shown naked to her suitor by a worthy and respectable matron, and so too a discreet man shows her suitor naked to the woman.[3] We laughed at this custom and condemned it as foolish, but they themselves marvel at the notable folly of other nations. In buying a pony, where there is just a little money involved, people in other nations are so cautious that though the animal is practically naked they will not buy until they have taken off the saddle and removed all the harness lest they conceal some sore. Yet in choosing a wife, a choice on which hangs lifelong pleasure or disgust, the same people are so careless that while the rest of her body is covered with clothes they judge the whole woman from one handbreadth, only her face being visible, and take her to themselves even though there is a high chance that two will find each other unattractive. Not every

---

1 [marginal note] Marriages.
2 [marginal note] Not very modest, but not so impractical either.
3 *The woman ... woman* Plato advocates this practice in his *Laws*.

man is so wise as to care only for the woman's character, and even wise men find good looks no small enhancement of the mind's virtues. Certainly a deformity hidden beneath these coverings may be so foul that it alienates a man's mind from his wife, bodily separation being no longer possible. If such a deformity comes by chance after the marriage contract, each must endure his own fate; but until then the law should protect him against being taken in by deceit.

This provision was all the more urgent, because the Utopians are the only people in that part of the world who are satisfied with one wife; marital bonds are seldom broken except by death, though on rare occasions a marriage may also end because of adultery or an intolerable offensiveness in the mate's disposition.[1] When either spouse is thus offended, the Council gives permission to take another mate while the rejected partner lives in disgrace and perpetual celibacy. But the Utopians think it wrong to divorce a wife because of some physical problem for which she is in no way to blame. They think it cruel to abandon anyone in need of comfort; if that sort of behavior were condoned, there would be little protection against the insecurities of age, which brings disease and is itself a disease.

But sometimes, when a married couple does not accord in dispositions and both find others with whom they hope they might live more agreeably, they part by mutual consent and contract fresh unions. This may not be done without the permission of the Council, which forbids divorce until it and the spouses have carefully reviewed the matter. Even then, it is reluctant to give consent, knowing that to feed hopes of remarriage is hardly a way to reinforce the marital bond.

Those who break that bond are punished by the strictest slavery. If both parties to an adultery were married, the injured spouses, if they so desire, may divorce their mates and marry each other or whomever they wish. If one of them still feels affection for the adulterous mate, the marriage shall continue in force if such a spouse is willing to accompany and share the labor of the one now condemned to slavery. Sometimes the penitence of the one partner and the dutiful persistence of the other move the Governor's compassion and they are freed. But those who repeat the offence risk being executed.

For other offences there is no fixed legal penalty, but in each case the Council appoints a punishment according to the seriousness of

---

1 [marginal note]   Divorce.

the crime.[1] Husbands chastise their wives, and parents discipline their children unless the offence is so monstrous that public punishment would serve public morality. Generally the worst offences are punished by slavery, since slavery is no less painful than death to the offender. Besides, putting criminals to work is far more advantageous to the state than slaughtering them forthwith. If they rebel and kick against this treatment, unrestrained by prison or fetter, then they are put to death like untamable beasts. If they are patient, however, they are not entirely without hope, for if, tamed by long misery, they show a penitence testifying that they are sorrier for their sin than for their punishment, then sometimes by the prerogative of the Governor and sometimes by the resolution of the people their slavery is either lightened or ended. Trying to tempt another into debauchery is as punishable as the act itself, for in all offences they count the deliberate and open attempt equal to the deed,[2] thinking that failure ought not to excuse one who wanted to succeed.

Utopians are very fond of fools. They think it a great disgrace to insult them, but there is no prohibition against taking delight in their fooling, for this benefits the fools themselves.[3] If anyone is too stern and morose to be amused by what fools do or say, the Utopians do not trust him to take on the care of one, fearing he might not treat the fool with enough indulgence.

To mock someone for a deformity or the loss of a limb they think shames the mocker, not the one mocked; it is stupid to find fault with something not in our power to avoid. Although they think it a sign of sluggish thick-wittedness not to try to preserve natural beauty through exercise and the like, for them it is a blameworthy presumption to pretty oneself up by putting paint on the skin.[4] Experience shows that no external loveliness recommends wives to husbands as much as do honor and integrity; though some men are won by pretty looks, only virtue and obedience make love endure.

The Utopians discourage crime not by punishment alone but also by giving honors and rewards that can incite citizens to do good

---

1 [marginal note] Degrees of punishment left to magistrates.
2 [marginal note] The penalty for soliciting to lewdness.
3 [marginal note] Pleasure derived from fools.
4 [marginal note] Artificial beauty.

deeds.[1] Thus they set up in the marketplace statues of those who have served the commonwealth well, so that their admirable acts might be remembered and their glory might inspire their descendents to virtue.

He that campaigns for votes is forbidden ever to hold any office.[2] Utopians live in mutual affection and goodwill, for no magistrate is haughty or formidable; they are called and indeed act like fathers.[3] Respect is willingly paid to them, as it should be, but it is not exacted from the unwilling. The Governor himself is not distinguished by a robe or a crown,[4] only by the handful of grain he carries, just as the high priest's mark is the wax candle borne before him.[5]

They have very few laws; a populace so well educated needs only a few.[6] The chief fault they find with other nations is that their almost numberless laws and legal commentaries are still not enough for them. They themselves think it most unfair to bind anyone by laws too many to read or too obscure to understand. Moreover, they utterly banish all lawyers, who use cleverness and cunning in handling cases and arguing legal points.[7] They think it best for everyone to plead his own cause and tell the judge the same thing he would tell an attorney. There is less ambiguity, and the truth is more readily determined, when one who has not been taught deception by a lawyer conducts his own case. The judge thoughtfully weighs each statement and helps the more naïve deal with accusations by the crafty.

It's unlikely that such practices would be adopted in other countries, with their mass of overcomplicated laws. In Utopia, everyone is an expert in the laws because, as I have said, they have very few of them and because for them a law's most obvious meaning is thought the most likely to be the most just. Since all laws are there mainly to remind citizens of their duty, they say, a refined and obscure meaning would remind only those few who could figure it out, whereas laws with a simple and obvious sense are clear to everyone. As for the common people (that is, the most numerous and most in need

---

1   [marginal note]   Citizens to be animated by rewards for good conduct.
2   [marginal note]   Running for office condemned.
3   [marginal note]   Magistrates held in honor.
4   [marginal note]   Dignity of the ruler.
5   *only by ... him*   The sheaf of grain symbolizes prosperity, as the candle symbolizes vision.
6   [marginal note]   Few laws.
7   [marginal note]   The useless crowd of lawyers.

of instruction), what difference would there be between having no law and having one that must be interpreted by experts? Since no one can master the meaning of such laws without much instruction and extensive debate, the wits of the common folk are too untrained, and their lives not long enough—granted their need to work for a living—for them to do so.

These virtues of the Utopians have moved those neighbors who are free and independent (the Utopians long ago having delivered many of them from tyrants) to borrow magistrates from them—some for a year, others for five. When their terms are up they escort them home with praise and honor and then return with their successors. Certainly such nations make very good provision for their own commonwealths; they recognize how much—prosperity or ruin—depends on the character of magistrates. How could they make a wiser choice than by choosing from those who will not leave the path of honesty for a bribe (since money will be no good to them after they return home) and who cannot be influenced either by partiality or animosity towards anyone (since everyone is a stranger to them). In every place where they hold sway over judgment, though, favoritism and greed instantly destroy the justice that is the strongest sinew of a commonwealth.

Utopians regard the peoples who fetch their magistrates from Utopia as "allies"; those they assist in any way they call "friends." They never make treaties with other nations, because the latter so often make them only to break them again.[1] What is the use of a treaty, they wonder; did Nature herself not sufficiently bind one person to another? If someone has no regard for Nature, can he really be expected to honor words? Utopians hold this opinion chiefly because in those parts of the world treaties and covenants between princes are observed with such little faith. Europeans, of course, and especially where the faith and religion of Christ prevails, everywhere consider the majesty of treaties holy and inviolable.[2] This respect arises in part from the justice and goodness of kings and in part from a reverence for and fear of popes, who not only carry out their own promises most conscientiously but also command all other rulers to keep their

---

1   [marginal note]   Treaties.

2   *Europeans ... inviolable*   Ironic—in fact, the rulers of the time, as well as the two most recent Popes (Alexander VI and Julius II), were notorious for breaking treaties.

vows, compelling the unruly by pastoral censure and stern rebuke. They rightly think it particularly reprehensible if those who are specially called the faithful do not faithfully keep their word.

In that New World, which is almost as far removed from ours by the Equator as their character and life are unlike our own, nobody relies on treaties. For the more numerous and binding are the ceremonies with which a treaty is tied and bound in those places, the more quickly is it dissolved; people quibble over the meaning of phrases that they have sometimes cunningly devised precisely to prevent themselves from being tied so strongly that they cannot escape, thus allowing themselves to break both the treaty and their word. If such cunning, fraud, and deceit were found in the contracts of individuals, men would condemn them as sacrilegious and deserving the gallows, although the same men would proudly advise kings to use the same methods. Such men must think either that all justice is merely a low and plebeian virtue, far below the majesty of kings, or that it has at least two forms. One goes on foot, creeping on the ground, fit only for the common sort and too shackled ever to overstep its bounds; the other is the virtue of kings, both grander and less onerous than that of ordinary folk, to which everything is permitted except what it doesn't want to do anyway.

The customs of kings who observe their treaties so badly explain, I suppose, why the Utopians make none; perhaps if they lived in Europe they would change their minds. But they think that, even if alliances are faithfully observed, it is a pity to make them at all. For the result is that men think themselves born adversaries and enemies of one another (as though nations divided by a mere hill or a river were joined by no natural bond) and that they are right in aiming to destroy each other unless a treaty were there to prevent it. Yet even after a treaty is made, friendship does not follow, for the right to pillage each other remains unless it is carefully, explicitly prohibited by the wording. The Utopians, on the other hand, think that nobody who has done you no harm should count as an enemy, that the fellowship that nature creates makes a treaty unnecessary, and that men are better and more firmly joined by good will than by covenants, better allied by affection than by words.

Chapter 8
Warfare

War may be brutish, but no brute is more passionate and eager for it than man. The Utopians regard it with utter loathing, and contrary to the fashion of almost all nations they count nothing so inglorious as glory won in battle. Though both men and women undergo military training on fixed days so as to be prepared, they do not go to war lightly. They will fight to protect their own territory, to drive an invading enemy out of their friends' lands, or to deliver an oppressed nation from the tyrant's yoke and bondage—a course prompted purely by human sympathy. They are willing to help their friends, not always merely to defend them but sometimes even to avenge injuries done them earlier. But they do this only if they are consulted before any step is taken, and they recommend that war should be declared only after they have approved the cause and a demand for restitution has been made in vain. This final step they are willing to take not only when a hostile force has carried out a raid but also when merchants from countries friendly with Utopia are wrongly accused under the pretence of justice in another country. Such was the origin of the war that the Utopians waged a little before our time on behalf of the Nephelogetes against the Alaopolitans.[1]

Some traders of the Nephelogetes suffered an injury, as they thought, under pretence of law, but rightly or wrongly, it was avenged by a fierce war. To this war the resources of neighboring nations were brought in to assist the power and intensify the resentment of both sides, until flourishing nations had been shaken or overthrown; the troubles were ended only by the surrender and subjection of the Alaopolitans. These yielded themselves to the rule of the Nephelogetes (for the Utopians were not fighting for their own interest), a people who had been, while the Alaopolitans were prosperous, not at all comparable to them in strength.

So you see how severely the Utopians punish wrongs done to their friends, even in money matters. But things are different when the wrongs are done to themselves. When defrauded of their goods anywhere, if there has been no violence their anger goes no farther than to suspend trade until some recompense arrives. It is not that

---

1   *Nephelogetes ... Alaopolitans*   More's own Greek coinages, meaning "People from the clouds" and "Nationless people."

they care less for their own citizens than for their friends, but they are more annoyed when their friends suffer financial loss than when they themselves do, for their friends' merchants, who lose their own property, suffer severely by the loss. Utopian citizens lose nothing more than some of what is held in common by all, and that must be plentiful at home, or it would not have been exported in the first place, and so no individual feels a loss. They therefore think it too cruel to avenge their loss by the death of many when that loss does not harm the life or the living of a Utopian citizen. But if any Utopian anywhere is wrongfully disabled or killed, whether by public sentence or private deed, they first ascertain the facts through diplomatic investigation and then, if the guilty persons are not extradited to them, they will not be appeased but immediately declare war. If the guilty persons are handed over, they punish them with death or slavery.

Utopians not only regret but are even ashamed of a victory that costs much blood, thinking it folly to purchase anything, however precious, at too high a price.[1] But if they overcome an enemy by stratagem and cunning, they exult beyond measure, holding a victory parade and erecting a trophy. They boast having acted valiantly and with manly prowess when their victory is one that no animal, but only a man could have won, being achieved through strength of mind; strength of body, they say, is for bears, lions, boars, wolves, dogs, and other wild beasts when they fight. Such animals are superior to us in strength and spirit but inferior in forethought and intelligence.

The Utopians' single object in fighting is to obtain the very thing that, had it been granted, would have prevented the war. But when it is not granted, they punish those on whom they lay the blame so severely that the perpetrators would be afraid to try anything like that again. This is the Utopians' chief interest, which they pursue directly, caring more to avoid danger than to win glory or honor.

As soon as war is declared, they arrange for posters carrying their official seal to be put up simultaneously in the most prominent spots of the enemy's territory. These promise large rewards to anyone who assassinates the enemy leader and smaller but still considerable sums for the heads of those named on the same posters, these being men whom, next to the leader himself, they hold responsible for the hostilities against them. Whatever reward they offer to anyone who kills one

---

1 [marginal note] Victory too dearly bought.

of these people they double for whoever brings one in alive. Indeed, they even offer the same rewards, with a guarantee of personal safety, to those whose names appear on the poster and who turn against their fellows. So before long their enemies suspect everyone else; among themselves, no one trusts or remains loyal to any other, and everyone is in a state of utter panic and real danger. It is known to happen that most of them, beginning with the king himself, are betrayed by those in whom they placed most trust—so easily do bribes incite men to commit any crime. Thus the Utopians place almost no limit on their offers of reward; knowing what a risk they ask people to run, they want the rewards to outweigh the risks. They thus promise not just a great deal of gold but also land in freehold that will bring in a great income—and they always keep their promises.

This policy of bidding for and purchasing an enemy, elsewhere condemned as base and degenerate, they think shows their wisdom, for they conclude great wars without actual battles. They also think it reflects well on their humanity and mercy, for by the death of a few guilty persons they purchase the lives of many harmless people who would have fallen in battle, and on both sides. They are as sorry for the common soldiers of the enemy as for their own, knowing that they do not go to war through their own choice but are, rather, driven to it by the madness of kings.

If this plan does not succeed, they plant seeds of dissension and foster strife by encouraging a brother of the king or one of his noblemen to hope he might take over the throne. If internal strife dies down, then they stir up the neighbors of their enemies by reviving some forgotten claims to dominion such as kings have always at hand and then promise their own assistance for the war. But although they supply money liberally, they are very reluctant to send their own citizens, whom they hold singularly dear, thinking each so valuable that they would not exchange any one of them for an enemy king. As for gold and silver, since they keep it all for this one use, they pay it out unhesitatingly, for they would live just as well if they spent it all. In addition to the riches that they keep at home, moreover, they have such a vast treasure abroad that many nations, as I said, are in their debt. Thus they hire mercenaries from all parts, especially from the country of the Zapoletes.[1]

---

1 *Zapoletes* "Busy sellers."

These people, who live five hundred miles to the east of Utopia, are rough, crude, and brave, fond of the woods and rugged mountains where they are bred.[1] They are a hardy race, able to endure heat, cold, and hard work, entirely without civilized refinement. They are not skilled in farming, are careless about the houses they inhabit and the clothes they wear, and occupied only with their flocks and herds. Living chiefly by hunting and plunder, they are born for warfare and zealously seek opportunities to fight. When such a chance arrives, they eagerly embrace it, and leaving the country in great numbers they offer themselves at a cheap rate to anyone who needs fighting men. The only art of living they know is the same one by which they seek their deaths. They fight hard and loyally for those who pay them. They bind themselves for no fixed period, and if the enemy offers them higher pay they switch sides, and then the day after that, if a little more is offered to them, they return to the side they had first taken. Seldom is there a war that does not see many of them in both armies, so it often happens that those bound by blood, as well as those serving in the same army and thus intimate with each another, soon find themselves on opposites sides and meet in battle. Then with fierce animosity, forgetting both kinship and friendship, they stab and destroy each other only because they were hired by opposing kings for a small sum of which they take such careful account that they are easily led to change sides by adding a penny to their daily pay. So quickly have they developed the habit of greed! And yet it profits them nothing, for what they get by exposing their lives they soon spend on riot and wretchedness.

This people will fight for the Utopians against any enemies whatsoever because paid more than they can get anywhere else. The Utopians, just as they seek good men to use, so they enlist these bad men to abuse. For when the need arises, they send them into great peril with the tempting bait of big promises. A large proportion never returns to claim their wages, but the survivors are honestly paid what has been promised in order to incite them to repeat similar deeds of daring. The Utopians do not care how many of them they lose, thinking that

---

1 [marginal note]   These people not unlike the Swiss. [Swiss mercenaries were hired by the rulers of several European countries at the time. To this day, popes continue to hire Swiss guards.]

it would benefit the whole human race if they could relieve the world of this abominable and shameful people.

Next in order of preference after these mercenaries, the Utopians employ the soldiers of the people for whom they are fighting; then auxiliary squadrons of other allies; and finally a contingent of their own citizens, out of whom they appoint some man of tried valor to command the entire army. They add two potential replacements; these hold no rank while he lives, but if he is taken prisoner or killed then one becomes, as it were, his heir and successor, and then he, if things fall out this way, is succeeded by the third.[1] Thus the death of the commander, the fortunes of war being always incalculable, will not bring the whole military into disorder.

Each city chooses from its volunteers. No one is forced to fight abroad against his will, because the Utopians are convinced that any-one who is timid by nature is unlikely to acquit himself manfully and may make his companions more timid. However, should any enemy assail their own country, they put the faint-hearted, provided that they are physically fit, on shipboard among the braver sort, or put them here and there to man the walls where they cannot run away. Thus the continual regard of their comrades, the looming threat of their enemies, and the impossibility of escape combine to overpower their timidity, and often extreme danger makes them brave.

Just as no one is forced to go fight abroad, so if wives want to go with their husbands to war, not only do the Utopians not forbid it, they even encourage and spur them on by praise. The pair leaves for battle together and wives fight next to their husbands, surrounded by their children, relations and connections, so that those to whom nature has given the strongest motive to help one another may be closest and offer mutual assistance. It is the greatest reproach for a husband to return without his wife, a wife without her husband, or a son without his father; so in hand-to-hand fighting, if the enemy stand his ground, the fight is long and desperate, and ends only when all are dead.

Though Utopians bend every effort not to have to fight themselves so long as they can finish the war by hiring substitutes, when personal service is inevitable they prove just as courageous in fighting as they had been prudent when trying to avoid it, not so fierce in the first on-

1   *They add … third*   Strategy practiced by the Spartans.

slaught as stubborn in the protraction and duration of the fight, more likely to be cut to pieces than to relent. The absence of that anxiety over a man's livelihood or his family's future, which everywhere else breaks the highest spirit, makes a Utopian hold his head high and disdain the foe. The Utopians' training in military discipline gives them confidence, moreover, and the good and sound opinions in which they have been trained from childhood, both in school and through good institutions of the commonweal, give them added courage. So although they do not hold their lives so cheap as to throw them away carelessly, neither do they hold them so excessively dear as to keep them at the price of shame when duty bids them sacrifice themselves.

When the battle is everywhere hottest, a picked band of young men who have sworn themselves to the mission seek out the enemy general, and openly assault or secretly ambush him.[1] They assail him from afar and at close range, as a long chain of men, with fresh comers taking the place of the exhausted, keep up the attack. Almost always, unless he saves himself by running away, he is killed or falls alive into Utopian hands. If the victory rests with the Utopians, they do not revenge themselves with blood, for they would rather take a defeated foe prisoner than kill him, and they never pursue the flying enemy without always keeping one division ready for engagement. Even if they win the battle with this reserve force after the rest of the army has been beaten, they prefer to let the whole hostile force escape rather than get into the habit of pursuing the foe in a disorderly way. They remember that one occasion, with most of their army beaten and routed, and while the enemy was flushed with victory and pursuing the fugitives in all directions, a few of their own number, held in reserve for emergencies, had suddenly counter-attacked the scattered enemy, who believing themselves quite safe were off their guard, and had changed the whole fortune of the battle. Thus the Utopians wrest back from the enemy's hand a certain and undoubted victory, conquering their seeming conquerors.

It is not easy to say whether the Utopians are more cunning in laying ambushes or more cautious in avoiding them. You would think them about to turn tail, when that is the last thing they intend. Then, when they do decide to retreat, you would imagine they were plan-

---

1   [marginal note]   The enemy general to be most fiercely attacked, so as to end the war sooner.

ning anything but that. For if they find themselves inferior in number or position, they noiselessly move away by night and set up camp elsewhere, or they evade the enemy by some stratagem, or by daylight withdraw so imperceptibly and in such regular order that it would be as risky to attack them in retreat as it would be if they were advancing. They carefully protect their camps by digging a deep and broad ditch, tossing aside the dirt. They do not use laborers for this. Rather, the soldiers make the ditch with their own hands, and so the whole army is kept at work except for those who keep armed watch in front of the rampart in case of emergencies. Thanks to the work of many hands they can create impressive fortifications, enclosing a large space with amazing speed.

They wear armor strong enough to ward off blows but so well adapted to their bodies' movements and gestures that they can even swim in it. (Learning to swim armed is part of their military training.)[1] The weapons they use at a distance are arrows, which they shoot with great strength and sureness of aim, both on foot and on horseback, while at close quarters they use not swords but axes, which deal a deadly blow either with blade or through sheer weight, depending on whether they are used to cut or thrust. They are ingenious in inventing weapons, carefully concealing them lest, if seen before needed, they become objects of laughter rather than instruments of war. In making them, their first criteria are maneuverability and ease of transport.

If they make a truce, they keep it so religiously that they will not break it under any provocation.[2] They do not ravage the enemy's country or burn his fields. Indeed, as far as possible they do not allow crops to be crushed by the feet of their men or horses, thinking them grown for their own benefit. They injure no non-combatant unless he is a spy. They keep intact any city that yields. They do not even plunder the ones they have stormed, but merely put to death the men who blocked a surrender and make slaves of the rest, leaving civilians unharmed. If they can locate those who had urged the city to yield they give them a share in the property of the condemned, presenting the rest of the confiscated goods to their auxiliaries; no Utopian touches the booty.

---

1   [marginal note]   The variety of their weapons.
2   [marginal note]   Truces.

When the war is over, they do not ask the friends for whom they have borne its cost to repay any of it, but rather they make the conquered pay reparations with cash, setting it aside for use in future wars, and also get them to hand over estates from which Utopia itself can get a large annual income, indefinitely.[1] They now have such varied sources of revenue in so many countries that the proceeds have grown to over seven hundred thousand ducats[2] a year. To administer these estates they send some of their own citizens, called Quaestors,[3] to live in grand style and play the part of great lords. Much is left over for the Utopians' common treasury, however, unless they prefer, as they often do, to give the defeated nation credit until the money is needed, and even then they almost never call in the whole sum. Out of these estates they confer a part on those who at their request undertake the dangerous mission that I described earlier. If any king arms himself against Utopia and is about to invade, they immediately march out in great strength beyond their own borders and meet him there, for they prefer not to fight on their own country, nor is any emergency so pressing as to make them let foreign auxiliaries into their island.

Chapter 9
The Religions in Utopia

There are different religions in different parts of the island and also within each city. Some worship the Sun, others the Moon, and yet others one of the planets. Some people reverence a man who was in former times conspicuous for virtue or glory, not just as *a* god, but also as the supreme God. But the most people, especially the wiser, do nothing of the kind, believing in one unknown Divine Power, eternal, incomprehensible, inexplicable, far beyond the reach of human intellect, diffused throughout the universe as a powerful force. Him they call Father, to Him alone they attribute the beginnings, the growth, the progress, the changes and the ends of all things, and to no other do they give divine honors.

---

1   [marginal note]   But today the victors foot most of the bill.
2   *ducats*   European gold coins of varying value depending on the nation of origin.
3   *Quaestors*   Agents.

Although all the others believe different things, they agree with the majority in thinking there is one Supreme Being to Whom we owe the creation and maintenance of the world. In their native language all call Him Mithra.[1] Different people define Him differently, however, each thinking that whatever they regard as supreme is that same nature, but all attribute the sum of all things to His unique power and majesty. Gradually, indeed, they are all beginning to depart from their variety of superstitions and are uniting in one religion that seems to surpass the rest in rationality. No doubt the other beliefs would have all disappeared long ago, had not some misfortune happened to those considering changing their religion. Their misfortune was read not as a work of chance but as the work of the deity they had been planning to leave and who wanted to punish their impiety against himself.

But when they heard from us the name of Christ, His teaching, His example, His miracles, and the no less wonderful constancy of the many martyrs whose blood, freely shed, has brought together so many nations in so many parts of the world, you cannot imagine how willing they were to embrace Christianity at once, either secretly inspired by God or because they found it similar to their own most influential beliefs. I think, though, that what carried a lot of weight was our report that Christ approved his disciples' communal way of life,[2] one that the truest Christian communities continue to practice.[3] Whatever it was that affected them, not a few agreed to adopt our faith and were baptized.

But among the four of us (all that remained of our company, two having died), I am sorry to say there was no priest. We gave the Utopians religious instruction, but not those sacraments that we believe only a priest can administer;[4] they understand what they are, however, and are eager to receive them. Indeed, they are even debating earnestly among themselves whether, if no Christian bishop were sent, they might choose one of their own number who could take on

---

1 *Mithra*   Persian god of truth and light.
2 *Christ ... way of life*   See Acts 2.44–5 and 4.32–5.
3 [marginal note]   Monasteries.
4 *those sacraments ... administer*   The administration of the Eucharist, Confession, Confirmation, Ordination, and Extreme Unction (the last rites of the Church before death) must be conducted by a priest, while Baptism and Marriage may be performed by non-clergy in extreme or emergency circumstances.

valid holy orders. It seemed that they would choose someone, but by the time I left they had not yet done so.

Utopians who do not accept Christianity nevertheless do not try to deter others from doing so or oppose their conversion. Only one of our community was disciplined while I was there. As soon as he had been baptized, and despite our protests, he began to speak publicly of Christianity with more zeal than discretion, so much so that he not only set our religion above any other but condemned outright all others as profane. He loudly called those of other faiths impious, sacrilegious, and worthy of eternal fire. After he had been preaching in this style for some time, he was arrested, not for despising their religion but for stirring up strife. Tried and convicted, he was sentenced to exile. Indeed, among the most ancient Utopian principles is one holding that no one should be made to suffer for his religion.[1]

Before his arrival at the island, King Utopus had heard that the natives were constantly quarrelling over religion. Such dissension among the various sects fighting for their country, he realized, gave him an opportunity to subdue them all. After he had won, he first declared everyone free to follow the religion of his own liking and even to strive to convert others, provided he did so modestly and peaceably, with reasonable arguments, and with no attempt bitterly to discredit the beliefs of others. Should his efforts fail, he was not to use violence and must refrain from abuse. Those arguing too vehemently would be subject to exile or enslavement. Utopus made this rule not merely for the sake of peace, so easily destroyed by constant religious wrangling and hatred, but also because he thought it in the interest of religion itself. He did not dogmatize concerning faith, thinking that perhaps God desires a varied and manifold worship and so has inspired different people with different views. In any case Utopus thought it arrogant and foolish to insist, with violence and threats, that everyone else must agree with what you believe to be true. He quickly perceived, moreover, that if one religion is true and the others false, then, if religious questions are dealt with reasonably and moderately, by its own natural force truth will emerge into clear visibility. But if such matters are to be decided by force and armed violence, he thought, then the best and holiest religion would be overwhelmed by false ones, like grain overtaken by thorns and bushes, for the worst men are always

---

1 [marginal note]   Men must be drawn to religion by its merits.

the most obstinate. So he left the matter open, making it clear that all were free to decide what to believe. The one rule on which he insisted unrelentingly was that no one should sink so far beneath the dignity of human nature as to believe that the soul dies with the body or that mere chance, and not divine providence, rules the world.

This is why Utopians believe that after this life our vices are punished and virtues rewarded; if anyone thinks otherwise they do not regard him as even human, seeing that he has debased the lofty nature of his soul to that of a brute. Still less do they count him as a citizen, for as far as he dared he would thumb his nose at their laws and customs. No one, after all, can doubt that such a person would attempt either to evade by craft the common laws of his country or to break them by violence so as to serve his greed; he would have nothing to fear but the law and no hope beyond the grave. So the Utopians forbid anyone of this mind to hold office; they do not entrust him with any public function and regard him as having a mean and low disposition. They do not punish him in any way, however, convinced that people cannot help what they believe. They neither use threats to make him disguise his views nor allow deceptions or lies in the matter, for they hate mendacity almost as much as they hate actual wrongdoing. They forbid such a person to argue for his opinion publicly, but they encourage him to do so in front of priests and citizens of weight and importance, convinced that such madness will in the end yield to reason.

Another group of people, on the other hand, and a fairly large one, believes that even animals have immortal souls, although not comparable to ours in dignity and not destined for an equal happiness.[1] The Utopians do not find such people bad, and even think that there is something to be said for such a belief. Almost all are absolutely convinced that human bliss in the afterlife will be measureless, so that although they lament everyone's illness, they regret the death of no one unless they see him leave life anxiously or reluctantly. That they take as a very bad omen, as though the unwilling soul, without hope and with a guilty conscience, had a secret premonition of impending punishment. Besides, they think, God will not be pleased by the arrival of one who, when summoned, does not gladly hasten to obey but is drawn unwillingly. Horrified whenever they see this kind of

---

1 [marginal note]   A strange opinion on the souls of animals.

death, they carry the departed to burial in melancholy silence, and then after praying that God might be merciful to the soul and graciously pardon its infirmities, they lay the corpse in the ground. On the other hand, over one who has died full of cheer and good hope, they do not mourn but attend the funeral with singing and affection, commending the soul to God. Then, with more reverence than sorrow, they burn the body[1] and on the spot erect a pillar inscribed with the virtues of the deceased. On returning home they speak of the person's character and deeds, no part of which is more frequently or gladly mentioned than the cheerful death.

They think this memorial to virtue both the best way to inspire the living to good deeds and the best way to honor the dead, who they think are present when talked about, even though invisible to weak mortal sight. For it would be inconsistent with the bliss of the departed not to be able to go where they please, and it would be ungrateful of them absolutely to reject all desire of revisiting their friends, to whom they were bound during their lives with mutual love and affection (which, like other good things, the Utopians believe does not diminish in the good but even increases posthumously). Thinking that their dead move among them, witnessing their words and actions, Utopians go about their business confident of their protection and convinced that the presence of their ancestors keeps them from all dishonesty.

They utterly despise and mock fortune-telling and all the superstitious divinations taken so seriously in many other places. But miracles, which occur without Nature's assistance, they revere as manifestations of divine power; such, they say, often occur in Utopia. Sometimes when in the midst of great danger they pray publicly for a sign, which they confidently expect and receive.

They think that to contemplate Nature and praise God in His works is a service acceptable to Him. There are some, and not so very few, who for religious reasons give up learning, pursue no science, and take no leisure, but pour themselves into work and other good deeds in order to win happiness after death.[2] Some tend the sick, others repair roads, clean out ditches, rebuild bridges, dig turf, sand and stone, fell and cut up trees, or cart wood, grain, or other materi-

---

1   *burn the body*   Before the nineteenth century Christians did not practice cremation.
2   [marginal note]   The active life.

als into the cities. They serve not only the public but also individuals, working harder than slaves. If anywhere there is a task so rough, hard, and repulsive that most are deterred by the toil, disgust, and despair involved, these people gladly and cheerfully claim it for themselves. Engaged in endless hard work, and claiming no credit, they secure leisure for others, neither denigrating other people's lives nor extolling their own. The more they perform like slaves, the more everyone honors them.

These people are of two sorts, with differing opinions and practices. One group includes those who remain single, abstaining not only from sex but also from meat and even, in some cases, all animal food. They completely reject this world's pleasures as harmful and focus only on the life to come, hoping to obtain it soon, by prayer and labor; in the meantime, they are cheerful and lively. Those of the other sort are just as fond of hard labor, but they prefer marriage to the single life. They do not despise the comfort that marriage brings, and think that they owe it to nature to labor, and owe it to their country to have children. They refuse no pleasure that does not interfere with their work, eating meat only because they believe it makes them stronger for their tasks. Most Utopians think this group wiser and the other one holier. If the holier sect tried to defend their preference for celibacy and a hard life with arguments drawn from reason, most would laugh them to scorn; but since they say that their faith prompts them, other Utopians look up to and revere them. (Utopians are exquisitely careful not to jump to conclusions over any point of religion.) Such, then, are these who in their language are given a special name, Buthrescae, or "the particularly religious."

Utopian priests are people of great holiness, so there are very few of them, not more than thirteen in each city, with the same number of churches. When Utopians go to war, seven priests accompany the army, and seven substitutes are appointed until the priests return and take up their former duties. The substitutes then return to their earlier tasks until the priests die, after which they succeed to their places. Until then they assist the Bishop, who is the head of all. Like other officials, priests are elected by secret ballot, so as to prevent politicizing the process, and winners are then ordained by their colleagues. They preside over worship, conduct religious ceremonies, and provide moral guidance. It is a great disgrace for a man to be summoned before them, or reproved for immorality. It is their part to give advice and admonition, whereas the Governor and the other magistrates correct and punish offenders. The priests do, however, excommunicate those whom they determine to be evildoers, and there is no punishment more dreaded. The excommunicated incur very great disgrace and are tortured by inner religious fear; even their bodies do not go scot-free, for unless they quickly satisfy the priests that they are truly repentant, the Council arrests and punishes them for impiety.

The education of the young is entrusted to the priests, whose first concern is not learning, but behavior and virtue. They take the greatest pains to instill into the minds of children, while they are still tender and pliable, attitudes that will help preserve the commonwealth. When firmly implanted, such principles will accompany them all their lives and strengthen the commonwealth, which decays only through vices rooted in distorted thinking. The priests have the most desirable women in the country for wives. (Women are not debarred from the priesthood, but they are only seldom chosen, and none except widows and the elderly.)[1] To no other office in Utopia is so much honor given as to the priesthood—so much so that even priests who have committed a crime are not tried before a public tribunal, but left to God and to themselves.[2] Utopians think it wrong to lay mortal hands on a priest, however guilty, who has been specially consecrated to God as a holy offering. It is easier for them to observe this custom because their priests are few and carefully chosen. Only seldom does anyone elevated to such dignity for being the best of the good, for nothing but virtue sink into corruption and vice. Even if priests do sin (which is bound to happen, given the fallibility of human nature), Utopians need not fear that this will bring ruin to the commonwealth, because priests are few and because their positions carry honor but no real power. Indeed, they keep the number of priests low in order to preserve the order's dignity; they think it hard to find many good enough for so honorable a post, one that requires a more than everyday virtue.[3]

Utopian priests are esteemed just as much in foreign countries as they are among their own people. When the armies are fighting, the

---

1   [marginal note]   Female priests.
2   [marginal note]   Unworthy priests.
3   [marginal note]   But what a crowd of them we have!

priests are to be found not far off, kneeling, dressed in their sacred vestments with hands outstretched to heaven, and praying first of all for peace, then for victory, but without bloodshed on either side.[1] When their own people are winning, the priests run among the combatants and restrain the fury of their own men against the routed enemy. The enemy soldiers see this and appeal to the priests, which is enough to save many lives. To touch their flowing garments protects the supplicant's goods from spoliation. This has brought them such veneration among all nations, and given them so real a majesty, that they have saved their own citizens from the enemy as often as they have protected the enemy from their own men. It has even happened that after the Utopians' own line was broken and things looked grim, while they were retreating and the enemy was rushing on, the priests intervened and brought an end to the carnage, and the armies parted and settled on equal terms. For never was there any nation so savage, cruel, and barbarous that it has not regarded their bodies as sacred and inviolable.

They keep as holy days the first and the last of each month, and also the first and last days of the year, which they divide into months.[2] These they measure by the orbit of the moon, just as they determine the year by the course of the sun. In their language they call the first days Cynemernes, and the last days Trapemernes, which may be interpreted as "First Feasts" and "Last Feasts." Their churches are fine sights, elaborate in workmanship and able to hold vast congregations—a necessity, granted that there are so few of them.[3] They are all fairly dark, not because of the builders' ignorance but because the priests think that dazzle makes the thoughts wander, whereas sparse and dim light concentrates the mind and encourages earnest devotion.

As I have said, not everyone has the same religion, and yet because all the different faiths tend to the same end, the worship of the Divine Nature, nothing is seen or heard in the churches that does not seem to agree with this common belief. If any sect has a rite of its own, its adherents perform it within the walls of their own houses. No image of God is seen in a church, therefore, so that all may be free to conceive

---

1 [marginal note]   O priests far more holy than our own!
2 [marginal note]   Holidays observed by the Utopians.
3 [marginal note]   What their churches are like.

of Him according to their own beliefs, in any likeness they please. The priests have no special name for God except "Mithra," by which word they agree to represent the one nature of the Divine Majesty, whatever it might be, and prayers are phrased so that everyone may recite them without offense.

The priests come to the church in the evening of the last day of the month or year, fasting, to thank God for the prosperity they have enjoyed in the past year or month. On the next day, or "first feast," they assemble at the churches in the morning to pray for happiness and prosperity in the following year or month. At a "last feast," before they go to church, wives fall at the feet of their husbands and children at those of their parents, confessing how they have offended, whether by losing something or carelessly performing some duty, and pray for pardon.[1] If any cloud of quarrel in the family has arisen, it is dispelled by this penance, so that with clear and pure minds they may attend the divine service; their religion forbids them to attend with a troubled conscience.[2] If aware of hatred or anger against anyone, they do not come to until reconciled and with cleansed hearts; otherwise they risk swift and severe punishment. When they reach the church, men go to the right, women to the left, and arrange themselves so that the males in each house sit in front of the father while the mother of the family sits behind the females. This system allows parents to make sure that those responsible for domestic discipline may observe every visible gesture. They also carefully see to it that everywhere the younger ones are placed in the company of the older, in order to keep children from spending in childish folly time they should pass in developing the respect for God that is the greatest (if not the only) stimulus to virtuous living.

The Utopians never sacrifice animals; they cannot believe that the Divine Being, who gave life to animals, delights in bloodshed and slaughter. They burn incense and other sweet savors, as well as a great many devotional candles. Not that they think these things add anything to the divine nature, any more than do the prayers of men, but they like this harmless kind of worship, and believe that these perfumes and lights and other ceremonies somehow uplift and impel them to a devotion to God's worship. The people wear white in

---

1   [marginal note]   The Utopian confession.
2   [marginal note]   But among us the worst sinners try to crowd closest to the altar.

church, and the priest wears vestments of various colors and wonderful design, but not of the costly material one might expect; these are not decorated with gold or precious stones but with different feathers, so cleverly and skillfully done that no costly material would have added to the value. According to the Utopians, the feathers, together with their arrangement on the priest's vestment, contain hidden mysteries with meanings carefully handed down by the priests and designed to remind Utopians of God's loving kindness to them, their own piety in return, and finally their duty to one another.

· When the priest thus arrayed first comes out of the inner sanctum, the people fall on the ground in reverence with such deep silence everywhere that the very character of the proceeding fills them with holy awe and feel that God is truly present. After remaining awhile on the ground, at a signal from the priest they rise; then they sing praises to God, often to the accompaniment of musical instruments fashioned differently, for the most part, than those in our part of the world.[1] Many of these surpass our own in sweetness of sound, though some are not as good. In one thing they are undoubtedly far ahead of us: all their music, whether instrumental or vocal, so renders and expresses the natural feelings, the sound suiting the matter (prayer, joy, supplication, trouble, mourning, or anger), and so communicates in the rising of the melody a certain understanding, that it wonderfully seizes, penetrates, and influences the minds of the hearers. At last the priest and people together repeat solemn prayers, each worded so that all may apply individually what all request together.

In these prayers, all recognize God as the Author of the creation, of government, and of every other blessing, thanking Him for all His gifts particular for the favor of life in the happiest of commonwealths and for the truest religion. If this is mistaken, or if there is anything better of which God approves more, then may He of His goodness bring them to its knowledge, for they are ready to follow in whatever direction He may lead. If the Utopian system is the best, however, and one's religion the truest, then may God grant steadfastness in the same and bring all others to the same way of living and the same understanding—unless God in His wisdom prefers a variety of religions. Finally they pray that He will grant an easy death, however soon, or late. But if it is God's will, they are much readier to die a hard death

---

1 [marginal note] Utopian music.

and go to God than to be kept for long away from Him by a prosperous course of life. After this prayer, the people fall down on the ground again. Then, after an interval, they rise and go away to dinner, and the rest of the day they pass in games and military training.

Now I have described to you, as truly as I could, the constitution of that commonwealth, which I think is not only the best but indeed the only one that deserves the name "commonwealth." For everywhere else, although people talk freely of the common good they think only of their own, whereas there, where there is no private property, citizens seriously care for the commonweal. No wonder: in other countries, who doesn't know that he has to look out for himself? If he doesn't, no matter how much the community as a whole may flourish, he will die of hunger, and so necessity compels him, he believes, to think of himself rather than of others.

In Utopia, on the other hand, where everything is shared, no one fears not having enough, provided the common warehouses are well filled. The distribution of good things is not ungenerous, and there are no poor people or beggars: though nobody can have just anything he wants, everyone is rich. For what greater wealth can there be than to live in joy and peace, with no fear for the future, untroubled about food, not harassed by the querulous demands of his wife, not afraid for his son's well-being or worried about his daughter's dowry, and thus without anxiety concerning his and his own, his wife, sons, grandsons, great-grandsons, great-great-grandsons and all the long succession of descendants to which people look forward?

Then recall that there is no less provision for those who have been laborers but are now unable to be such than for those who are still working. Here I would challenge anyone to compare the so-called justice practiced in other nations (among whom, I swear, I cannot discover a trace of justice or fairness) with the Utopian system. For what kind of justice is it for a nobleman or a goldsmith or a moneylender or any of those who do nothing (nothing of use to the commonwealth, anyway) to receive a grand and luxurious living in return for their leisure and pointless work? In the meantime, the day laborer, the carter, the smith, or the farmer, in return for continuous toil that beasts of burden could scarcely endure, and toil so essential that no state could last for a year without it, gets such a poor living and leads such a miserable life that the condition of beasts of burden might seem far preferable. For beasts do not have to work so incessantly, are not much worse fed, derive more pleasure from their lives, and have no fear for the future. The laborers not only must work here and now with little reward but are agonized by the thought of a helpless and indigent old age. Given that their daily wage does not even buy their daily bread, how could they possibly spare anything to put away for buying such bread when they are old?

Is it not unjust and ungrateful to lavish huge rewards on so-called gentlefolk, on goldsmiths, the idle, the parasites, the suppliers of empty pleasures? Is it not unjust to care nothing for those farmers, coal miners, day laborers, carters and smiths without whom there would be no commonwealth at all? But after such a system has used up laborers in their prime, and then, when they are weighed down by age and disease, and in their utter need, forgets all the benefits it has received from them it pays them back with a wretched death. Worse, every day the rich skim off part of the daily assistance to the poor, and not fraudulently but in ways sanctioned by the law itself. And so what was unjust to begin with—a pitiful allowance for those who deserve the best from the commonwealth—they have managed to make a complete travesty by enshrining their injustice in the laws they pass. So when I reflect on the state of all nations flourishing today, so help me God, I can see nothing but a conspiracy of the rich, seeking their own advantage under the name and pretext of the commonwealth.[1] They invent and devise all ways and techniques by which they may keep everything they have amassed by evil means and have no fear of losing their power to drive down wages and profit by the sweat and toil of the poor.

These sinister devices, as soon as the rich declare them to be in the public interest, even in the interest of the poor, finally become laws. But when these evil men, out of their insatiable greed, have divided among themselves what would have been enough for everyone, how far they fall short of the happiness of Utopia! When in Utopia all greed for money was abolished by abolishing money itself, what a mass of troubles was eliminated, and what a great crop of crimes was pulled up by the roots! For who does not know that fraud, theft, rob-bery, quarrels, disorder, strife, sedition, murder, treason, poisoning, avenged but not deterred by the daily executions, vanish with the

---

1 [marginal note]   Reader, note well!

death of money, and that fear, anxiety, worries, toils and watching will perish along with it? Although money is often thought to be the solution, take money away, and the problem itself disappears and dies away. To illustrate, imagine a barren year, with failed crops, in which many thousands have died of hunger. I'm sure that after the famine was over, if you searched the rich man's warehouses you would find so much grain that, had it been distributed to the poor, those killed by hunger and disease would not have even noticed the fury of the sky and soil. How easily might men get their living, if that much-lauded money, that grand invention meant to open the way to a living, was not itself the only barrier to our getting a living! Even the rich should see that it would be better not to lack necessities than to have a great heap of superfluities, better to escape the many troubles caused by need than be hemmed in by great riches. Nor do I doubt that caring for our own advantage or for the authority of our Savior Christ (Whose wisdom could not fail to know what is best, and Whose goodness would not advise what He knew not to be best) would long ago have brought the world to adopt the laws of this commonwealth had not one single monster, the chief and originator of all plagues, stood in the way—Pride.[1] She measures prosperity not by her own good but by the harm of others. She would not even want to be made a goddess if she had no poor wretches to lord it over. Let her prosperity vex and aggravate their poverty so long as their poverty amplifies and sets off her prosperity. This serpent of Hell slithers into human hearts and stops us, like a suckfish attached to a ship, from following life's better course, sticking on us too tightly to be easily pulled off.

Pride is too deeply rooted in us to be readily plucked out, so I rejoice that at least the Utopians have a system that I wish everyone everywhere would imitate. They have established institutions as the basis of their commonwealth that will produce the greatest possible happiness and that, as far as human foresight can tell, could last forever. At home they have pulled up the roots of ambition and faction, along with other vices, so there is no danger of trouble from the internal strife that has been the only cause for the ruin of many cities' well-established prosperity. So long as the Utopians preserve their internal harmony and keep institutions healthy, not all the envy of

---

1 [marginal note]   A striking phrase.

neighboring kings can shake or endanger that nation, although such has often been attempted—with no success.

When Raphael had finished his story, I was left thinking that not a few of that people's customs and laws were absurd—not only their method of waging war, their rites and religion, and their other institutions, but above all that which is the chief foundation of their entire system: their communal life with shared goods and no money. This alone utterly overthrows the nobility, magnificence, splendor, and majesty that are, in the opinion of the common people, the true glories and ornaments of a commonwealth. Yet I knew that he was wearied by telling his tale, and I myself had not had enough time to think it over. I doubted, too, whether he could brook any opposition to his views, particularly as I remembered how he had censured those who feared that they might not seem wise enough unless they could find fault with other men's thoughts. And so I praised the Utopian way of life, and also Raphael's account of it, and took him by the hand and led him in to supper, first saying that there would be time to think more deeply about these matters and to discuss them more fully. I hope that will indeed happen. In the meantime, while Raphael is in other ways a man of most undoubted learning, one with wide knowledge of the world, I cannot agree with all he said. And yet I readily admit that there are many features of the Utopian commonwealth that I can more easily wish for in our own societies than hope to see realized.

—1516

In Context

Illustration of Utopia

Ambrosius Holbein, *Map of the Island of Utopia*. This illustration appeared in the 1518 edition (the 1516 edition includes a less fully-developed illustration by an unknown artist).

Utopian Language

THE UTOPIAN ALPHABET
a b c d e f g h i k l m n o p q r s t u x y
A QUATRAIN IN THE UTOPIAN LANGUAGE
Vtopos ha Boccas peula chama.
polta chamaan
Bargol he maglomi baccan
ſoma gymnoſophaon
Agrama gymnoſophon labarem
bacha bodamilomin
Voluala barchin heman la
lauoluola dramme pagloni.

A Literal Translation of These Verses

Utopus it was who redrew the map,
    And made me an island instead of a cape:
Alone among nations resplendent I stand,
    Making virtue as plain as the back of your hand—
Displaying to all without argumentation
    The shape of a true philosophical nation.
Profusely to all of my own store I give;
    What is shown me that's better, I gladly receive.

Poems in the Utopian Tongue

The first poem in Utopian was published with the 1516 edition of *Utopia*, together with a translation into Latin. Several later writers found it amusing to write in Utopian, although not using the original Utopian alphabet. For an example of Utopian in prose, see François Rabelais's *Pantagruel*.

Henry Peacham, epigrammatist and author of a book on drawing, contributed to the many friendly but mocking poems that prefaced *Coryate's Crudities* (1611) by Thomas Coryate of Odcomb, famous for his foreign travels and sometimes clownish behavior. Here the joke is the imaginary language that more or less lists real places:

In the Utopian Tongue

Ny thalonin ythsi Coryate lachmah babowans
O Asiam Europam Americ-werowans
Poph-himgi Savoya, Hessen, Rhetia, Ragonzie
France, Germanien dove Anda-louzie[1]
Not A-rag-on[2] ô Coryate, ô hone vilascar
Einen trunk Od-combe ny Venice Berga-mascar.

John Taylor, "The Water Poet," was by profession a waterman, ferrying customers up and down the Thames, and by avocation the author of many comic tracts and poems. One of his poems in Utopian appears in *Laugh, and be Fat* (1612), reprinted in his 1630 *Works*. It too is about Thomas Coryate and incorporates fragments of English words, usually as implied insults:

The Utopian Tongue

Thoyton Asse Coria Tushrump[3] codsheadirustie,
Mungrellimo whish whap ragge dicete tottrie,
Mangelusquem verminets nipsem barelybittimsore
Culliandolt travellerebumque, graiphone trutchmore.

---

1 *Anda-louzie* Andalusia, in Spain, but also "And lousy"—having lice.
2 *A-rag-on* Aragon (part of Spain) but also not even wearing a rag, naked.
3 *Thoyton Asse Coria Tushrump* "Thomas Coryat" is embedded in the nonsense words.

Pusse per mew (Odcomb) gul abelgrik foppery shig shag
Cock a peps Comb[1] sottishamp, Idioshte momulus[2] tag rag.

A poem by Taylor from *Odcomb's Complaint* (1613; for sale, says
the title page, in Utopia) and reprinted in 1630 comes right after a
poem in the "Barmooda" tongue (ostensibly the language of the pigs
found by the first European visitors to Bermuda). It is also on Coryate
and incorporates place names and words from real languages:

Epitaph in the Utopian tongue

Nortumblum callimumquash omystoliton quashte burashte,
Scribuke woshtay solusbay per ambulatushte;
Grekay sons Turkay Paphay zums Jerusalushte.
Neptus esht Ealors Interremoy diz Dolorushte,
Confabuloy Odcumbay Prozeugmolliton tymorumynoy,
Omulus oratushte paralescus tolliton umbroy.

The Same in English,
Translated by Caleb Quishquash, an Utopian Born
and Principal Secretary to the Great Adelontado of Barmoodoes

Here lies the wonder of the English nation,
Involved in Neptune's brinish vasty maw:
For fruitless travel, and for strange relation,
He passed and repassed all that e're eye saw.
Odcomb produced him; many nations fed him,
And worlds of writers, through the world have spread him.

---

1   *Cock a peps Comb*   A phrase incorporating "cockscomb."
2   *momulus*   A "momulus" would be a little "Momus," traditional Greek god of mockery.

from Thomas More's Correspondence

The following selections from Thomas More's letters make reference to *Utopia*. They illustrate the circumstances of the work's publication as well as the social context in which it was written.

a. from Letter to Erasmus (3 September, 1516)[1]

More sends his very best greetings to Master Erasmus.

I am sending you my *"Nowhere,"*[2] which is nowhere well written. I have added a prefatory epistle to my friend, Peter. I know from experience that I do not have to tell you to give proper attention to everything else. I have delivered your letter to the Venetian ambassador, who, it appears, was very well disposed to receive your New Testament....

b. from Letter to Erasmus (c. 20 September, 1516)[3]

More sends his very best greetings to Erasmus.

I received your letter from Calais, and am happy to hear that you had a pleasant voyage. The Provost of Cassel, now on a diplomatic mission to our country, told me that you had arrived safe at Brussels before he left home....

Some time ago I sent you my *Nowhere;* I am most anxious to have it published soon and also that it be handsomely set off with the highest of recommendations, if possible, from several people, both intellectuals and distinguished statesmen.... I am also anxious to know if you have shown it to Tunstall, or at least described it to him, as I think you have done, and which I do prefer. For then he will gain a twofold delight; your account will make the work appear to have a more elegant style than it really has, and also you will save him the job of reading it himself. Farewell.

---

1 *Letter to Erasmus*   Translated by Marcus Haworth, 1961.
2 *"Nowhere"*   More's initial choice for the title of *Utopia*.
3 *Letter to Erasmus*   Translated by Marcus Haworth, 1961.

c. Letter to Erasmus (31 October, 1516)[1]

Thomas More sends greetings to his friend, Master Erasmus.

My answer, dear Erasmus, is a little tardy, because I was anxious to get some definite information to send on to you from Urswick about that horse for you; but that has been impossible, since he is gone on a business trip several miles from London and has not as yet returned. I expect him any day now, and as soon as he gets back, the matter will be taken care of. The money you had left with me, I am sure, has been paid over to our friend, Gilles, as I have received a communication from my agent in Antwerp, saying that he would make prompt payment. I could not entrust this bearer with the letters from Basel, which you sent me some time ago to peruse; but I will send them shortly, as soon as I hit upon someone to burden with a large bundle. Bedill showed me the letter from the Bishop of Basel to the Archbishop of Canterbury, and also the Archbishop's response; both were the original copies. The latter, however, was much too much the original; it was so smeared with words struck out or written in as to be not at all legible except to the one who wrote it, and perhaps not even to him.

Our two letters encouraging Latimer to spend a month or two with the Bishop of Rochester reached him too late; he had already made up his mind to go to Oxford and could not possibly be persuaded to postpone his trip for the time being. You know how these philosophers regard their own decisions as immutable laws; I suppose from a love of consistency. He does like your rendering of the New Testament very much, although you are too punctilious to suit him. He does not like the fact that you have retained the word "Sabbath," and other similar points, which you did not think necessary to change, or did not dare to do so. However, he does not admit of any word at all that would be foreign to Roman ears. I approved of his criticism insofar as Hebrew customs and practices would permit. However, I urged him to note down the various words for which he prefers a different rendering and to send them on to you, along with his criticism; and I think he will do that. This interest of his, I know, will make you very happy.

---

1   *Letter to Erasmus*   Translated by Marcus Haworth, 1961.

There are other people, though, my dearest Erasmus, who have formed a conspiracy here in our country to read through your writings from quite a different point of view; and I find their dreadful plot disturbing. Therefore, do not be in a rush to publish a second edition of your works, as the time is ripe to take stock. Out of my loyalty and my anxiety for you I urge you, and I beg you to do at least this much—to revise and correct everything promptly so as to leave the very least opportunity for slander in any passage. Some very sharp-minded men have set their hearts upon making a careful search for such opportunities and will snap them up greedily. You want to know who these people are? I am reluctant, of course, to mention any names, for fear that your spirit be crushed by the frightening thought of such powerful enemies. However, I shall tell you anyhow, to put you more on your guard. The top-ranking Franciscan theologian, whom you know and to whom you gave honourable mention in your edition of Jerome, has picked a group of men who are of the same Order and made of the same stuff, and has hatched a plot with them, aimed at refuting any errors of yours he can find. To make this operation easier and more effective, they devised a scheme whereby they would divide up your works among themselves, read through each one with a critical eye, and then understand absolutely nothing of it all. So you see what a crisis is hanging over your head! You have got to work hard to condition your troops for facing this monstrous peril. You can be sure, Erasmus, this decision was reached at a council meeting of the elders, late at night, when they were well soaked. But the morning after, as I am told, with the effects of the wine slept off, they forgot, I guess, all about their resolution; since the decree was written in wine, it was now blotted out of their memory, and so they abandoned their proposal, and instead of reading, they went back to their begging, which experience had taught them to be a far more profitable enterprise.

It is worth noting how much everybody enjoys the *Epistolae Obscurorum Virorum;*[1] the educated take it as a joke, while the uneducated take it seriously and think that our laughter is caused by the style alone. While not defending the style, they do maintain that it is offset by the weighty contents, and under the crude scabbard lies a

---

[1] *Epistolae Obscurorum Virorum   Letters of Obscure Men*, a collection of satirical letters in Latin making fun of scholastic and monastic thought.

very handsome blade. It is unfortunate that the work does not have a different title! Then not even in a hundred years would the silly fools realize that the authors were sneering at them with a snout more obtrusive than that of a rhinoceros.

I am happy that my *Nowhere* meets the approval of my friend, Peter; if such men like it, I shall begin to like it myself. I am anxious to find out if it meets with the approval of Tunstall, and Busleiden, and your Chancellor; but their approval is more than I could wish for since they are so fortunate as to be top-ranking officials in their own governments, although they might be won over by the fact that in this commonwealth of mine the ruling class would be completely made up of such men as are distinguished for learning and virtue. No matter how powerful those men are in their present governments—and, true, they are very powerful—still they have some high and mighty clowns as their equals, if not their superiors, in authority and influence. I do not think that men of this calibre are swayed by the fact that they would not have many under them as subjects, as the term is now used by kings to refer to their people, who are really worse off than slaves; for it is a much higher honour to rule over free people; and good men, such as they, are far removed from that spiteful feeling which desires others to suffer while they are well off themselves. I expect, therefore, that those men will also give their approval to my work, and I am very anxious to have it. However, if a deep conviction to the contrary has been implanted in their minds by satisfaction with their present good fortune, then your one vote will be more than adequate to influence my decision. To my way of thinking, we two are a crowd, and I think I could be happy with you in any forsaken spot.

Farewell, dearest Erasmus, more precious to me than my own eyes!

I have succeeded in getting a more favourable letter from Maruffo; that seemed to me to be more convenient and more prudent than to bother the Bishop again about the same matter. Not that he would be unwilling to listen to anything, as long as it concerned you; but I do prefer to approach him with matters of greater import.

Hurriedly, from London, before dawn, All Hallows Eve.

d. from Letter to Cuthbert Tunstall[1] (c. November, 1516)[2]

Although all the letters I receive from you, my honoured friend, are pleasing to me, yet the one you last wrote is the most pleasing; for besides its eloquence and its friendliness—all your letters abound with these commendations—it gave me especial satisfaction by its praise of my *Commonwealth*[3] (would that it were as true as it is favourable). I asked our friend Erasmus to describe to your in conversation its theme, but forbade him to urge you to read the book. Not that I did not wish you to read it (nothing would have pleased me more) but I was mindful of your resolution not to take in hand any modern authors until you had sated yourself with reading the ancients—a task which, measured by the profit you have derived from them, is fully accomplished, but, measured by the love you bear them, will never come to an end. I feared that when the learned works of so many other authors could not engage your attention, you would never willingly descend to my trifles. Nor would you have done so, surely, unless you had been moved rather by your love of me than by the subject of the book. Wherefore, for having so carefully read through the *Utopia,* for having undertaken so heavy a labour for friendship's sake, I give you the deepest thanks, not diminished by your having found pleasure in the work. For this, too, I attribute to your friendship which has obviously influenced your judgment more than strict rules of criticism. However that may be, I cannot express my delight that your judgment is so favourable. For I have almost succeeded in convincing myself that you say what you think, for I know that you are far from all deceit, and I am not important enough to be flattered, and I love you too much to deserve mockery. So that if you have objectively seen the truth, I am overjoyed at your verdict; or if in reading you were blinded by your affection for me, I am no less delighted with your love, for vehement indeed must be that love if it can deprive Tunstall of his judgment....

---

1   *Cuthbert Tunstall*   Prominent member of the clergy (1474–1559). At the time of this letter, he was the Principal Clerk of the Chancery Court, a court of appeals (1516-22), and he was later appointed Bishop of Durham (1530-52 and 1553-59).

2   *Letter to Cuthbert Tunstall*   From Elizabeth Frances Rogers, ed., *St. Thomas More: Selected Letters*, 1961.

3   *Commonwealth*   I.e., *Utopia*.

e. from Letter to William Warham[1] (January, 1517)[2]

... Herewith I would beg your Lordship to accept a none too witty little book (the *Utopia*). It was written in undue haste, but a friend of mine, a citizen of Antwerp (Peter Gilles) allowed his affection to outweigh his judgment, thought it worthy of publication, and without my knowledge had it printed. Although I know it is unworthy of your high rank, your wide experience, or your learning, yet I venture to send it, relying on the generosity with which you habitually encourage all men's literary endeavours, and trusting to the favour I have always experienced from you. Thus I hope that even if the book pleases you but little, yet your good will may be extended to the Author. Farewell, my lord Archbishop.

from Thomas More, *A Dialogue of Comfort against Tribulation* (1534)[3]

> More makes reference in several other works to some of the central ideas of *Utopia*. Perhaps of greatest interest in this respect is *A Dialogue of Comfort against Tribulation*, excerpts from which appear below. It is worth emphasizing, however, that this work dates from 1534—almost twenty years after More finished his *Utopia*; it is therefore not possible with any confidence to draw conclusions about his beliefs at the time of writing *Utopia* based on the arguments made in this dialogue.

ANTHONY. ... No marvel, now, if good folk who fear God take occasion of great dread at so dreadful words, then they see the worldly goods fall to them. And some stand in doubt whether it be lawful for them to keep any goods or not. But evermore, in all those places of scripture, the having of the worldly goods is not the thing that is rebuked and threatened, but the affection that the haver unlawfully beareth to them. For where St. Paul saith, "they that will

---

1 *William Warham* Archbishop of Canterbury at the time of this letter (1504-32), William Warham (c. 1447-1532) was very generous in his gifts to scholars, and to Erasmus in particular.

2 *Letter to William Warham* As reproduced in Stapleton's *Life of More*, translated by P.E. Hallet, 1928.

3 *A Dialogue of Comfort against Tribulation* Modifications to obsolete language by Monica Stevens, 1951.

be made rich," he speaketh not of the having but of the will and desire and affection to have, and the longing for it. For that cannot be lightly without sin. For the thing that folk sore long for, they will make many shifts to get and jeopard themselves for.

And to declare that the having of riches is not forbidden, but the inordinate affection of the mind sore set upon them, the prophet saith, "If riches flow unto you, set not your heart thereupon."

And albeit that our Lord, by the said example of the camel or cable rope to come through the needle's eye, said that it is not only hard but also impossible for a rich man to enter into the kingdom of heaven, yet he declared that though the rich man cannot get into heaven of himself, yet God, he said, can get him in well enough....

VINCENT. ... But ... I cannot well perceive (the world being such as it is, and so many poor people in it) how any man can be rich, and keep himself rich, without danger of damnation for it.

For all the while he seeth so many poor people who lack, while he himself hath wherewith to give them. And their necessity he is bound in such case of duty to relieve, while he hath wherewith to do so—so far forth that holy St. Ambrose saith that whosoever die for default,[1] where we might help them, we kill them. I cannot see but that every rich man hath great cause to stand in great fear of damnation, nor can I perceive, as I say, how he can be delivered[2] of that fear as long as he keepeth his riches. And therefore, though he might keep his riches if there lacked poor men and yet stand in God's favour therewith, as Abraham did and many another holy rich man since; yet with such an abundance of poor men as there is now in every country, any man who keepeth any riches must needs have an inordinate affection unto it, since he giveth it not out unto the poor needy persons, as the duty of charity bindeth and constraineth him to.

And thus, uncle, in this world at this day, meseemeth your comfort unto good men who are rich, and are troubled with fear of damnation for the keeping, can very scantly serve.[3]

ANTHONY. Hard is it, cousin, in many manner of things, to bid

---

1 *die for default* Die of privation or neglect.
2 *delivered* I.e., relieved.
3 *meseemeth ... serve* I.e., it seems to me that your defence of good rich men, who are afraid of being damned for keeping their weath, is not sufficient to comfort them.

or forbid, affirm or deny, reprove or approve, a matter nakedly proposed and put forth; or precisely to say "This thing is good," or "This thing is evil," without consideration of the circumstances.

Holy St. Austine[1] telleth of a physician who gave a man in a certain disease a medicine that helped him. The selfsame man at another time in the selfsame disease took the selfsame medicine himself, and had of it more harm than good. This he told the physician, and asked him how the harm should have happened. "That medicine," quoth he, "did thee no good but harm because thou tookest it when I gave it thee not." This answer St. Austine very well approveth, because, though the medicine were the same, yet might there be peradventure[2] in the sickness some such difference as the patient perceived not—yea, or in the man himself, or in the place, or in the time of the year. Many things might make the hindrance, for which the physician would not then have given him the selfsame medicine that he gave him before....

ANTHONY. ... [C]ousin, men of substance must there be. For otherwise shall you have more beggars, perdy,[3] than there are, and no man left able to relieve another. For this I think in my mind a very sure conclusion: If all the money that is in this country were tomorrow brought together out of every man's hand and laid all upon one heap, and then divided out unto every man alike, it would be on the morrow after worse than it was the day before. For I suppose that when it were all equally thus divided among all, the best would be left little better then than almost a beggar is now. And yet he who was a beggar before, all that he shall be the richer for, that he should thereby receive, shall not make him much above a beggar still. But many a one of the rich men, if their riches stood but in movable substance, shall be safe enough from riches, haply for all their life after![4]

Men cannot, you know, live here in this world unless some one man provide a means of living for many others. Every man cannot have a ship of his own, nor every man be a merchant without a

---

1   *St. Austine*   St. Augustine.

2   *peradventure*   By chance.

3   *perdy*   Truly.

4   *But many ... after*   I.e., without goods to sell or wealth to invest, such rich men would no longer have the means to conduct their business.

stock. And these things, you know, must needs be had. Nor can every man have a plough by himself. And who could live by the tailor's craft, if no man were able to have a gown made? Who could live by masonry, or who could live a carpenter, if no man were able to build either church or house? Who would be the makers of any manner of cloth, if there lacked men of substance to set sundry sorts to work? Some man who hath not two ducats in his house would do better to lose them both and leave himself not a farthing, but utterly lose all his own, rather than that some rich man by whom he is weekly set to work should lose one half of his money. For then would he himself be likely to lack work. For surely the rich man's substance is the wellspring of the poor man's living. And therefore here would it fare by the poor man as it fared by the woman in one of Æsop's fables. She had a hen that laid her every day a golden egg, till on a day she thought she would have a great many eggs at once. And therefore she killed her hen and found but one or twain[1] in her belly, so that for a few she lost many.

from Erasmus, Letter to Ulrich von Hutten (23 July, 1519)[2]

The German author Ulrich von Hutten (1488-1523) is best known for his contributions to *The Letters of Obscure Men*, a satire mocking monastic thought which More greatly enjoyed. Hutten similarly admired More's work, but the two had never met. In 1519, a few years after the first publication of *Utopia*, Hutten asked Erasmus to describe More's personality, and Erasmus responded with enthusiasm, providing the following portrait of More's character, accomplishments, and small eccentricities.

Most illustrious Hutten, your love, I had almost said your passion for the genius of Thomas More,—kindled as it is by his writings, which, as you truly say, are as learned and witty as anything can possibly be,—is, I assure you, shared by many others; and moreover the feeling in this case is mutual; since More is so delighted with what you have written, that I am myself almost jealous of you. It is an example of what Plato says of that sweetest wisdom, which excites much more

---

1   *twain*   Two.
2   *Letter to Ulrich von Hutten*   Translated by Francis M. Nichols, 1917.

ardent love among men than the most admirable beauty of form. It is not discerned by the eye of sense, but the mind has eyes of its own, so that even here the Greek saying holds true, that out of Looking grows Liking; and so it comes to pass that people are sometimes united in the warmest affection, who have never seen or spoken to each other. And, as it is a common experience, that for some unexplained reason different people are attracted by different kinds of beauty, so between one mind and another, there seems to be a sort of latent kindred, which causes us to be specially delighted with some minds, and not with others.

As to your asking me to paint you a full-length portrait of More, I only wish my power of satisfying your request were equal to your earnestness in pressing it. For to me too, it will be no unpleasant task to linger awhile in the contemplation of a friend, who is the most delightful character in the world. But, in the first place, it is not given to every man to be aware of all More's accomplishments; and in the next place, I know not whether he will himself like to have his portrait painted by any artist that chooses to do so. For indeed I do not think it more easy to make a likeness of More than of Alexander the Great, or of Achilles; neither were those heroes more worthy of immortality. The hand of an Apelles is required for such a subject, and I am afraid I am more like a Fulvius or a Rutuba than an Apelles.[1] Nevertheless I will try to draw you a sketch, rather than a portrait, of the entire man, so far as daily and domestic intercourse has enabled me to observe his likeness and retain it in my memory. But if some diplomatic employment should ever bring you together, you will find out, how poor an artist you have chosen for this commission; and I am afraid you will think me guilty of envy or of wilful blindness in taking note of so few out the many good points of his character.

To begin with that part of him which is least known to you, in shape and stature More is not a tall man, but not remarkably short, all his limbs being so symmetrical, that no deficiency is observed in this respect. His complexion is fair, his face being rather blonde than pale, but with no approach to redness, except a very delicate flush, which lights up the whole. His hair is auburn inclining to black, or if you like it better, black inclining to auburn; his beard thin, his eyes

---

1   *Fulvius ... Apelles*   Fulvius and Rutuba are gladiators referred to in Horace's *Satires*, while Apelles was a renowned ancient Greek painter.

a bluish grey with some sort of tinting upon them. This kind of eye is thought to be a sign of the happiest character, and is regarded with favour in England, whereas with us black eyes are rather preferred. It is said, that no kind of eye is so free from defects of sight. His countenance answers to his character, having an expression of kind and friendly cheerfulness with a little air of raillery. To speak candidly, it is a face more expressive of pleasantry than of gravity or dignity, though very far removed from folly or buffoonery. His right shoulder seems a little higher than his left, especially when he is walking, a peculiarity that is not innate, but the result of habit, like many tricks of the kind. In the rest of his body there is nothing displeasing, only his hands are a little coarse, or appear so, as compared with the rest of his figure. He has always from his boyhood been very negligent of his toilet, so as not to give much attention even to the things, which according to Ovid are all that men need care about.[1] What a charm there was in his looks when young, may even now be inferred from what remains; although I knew him myself when he was not more than three and-twenty years old; for he has not yet passed much beyond his fortieth year. His health is sound rather than robust, but sufficient for any labours suitable to an honourable citizen; and we may fairly hope, that his life may be long, as he has a father living of a great age, but an age full of freshness and vigour.

I have never seen any person less fastidious in his choice of food. As a young man, he was by preference a water-drinker, a practice he derived from his father. But, not to give annoyance to others, he used at table to conceal this habit from his guests by drinking, out of a pewter vessel, either small beer almost as weak as water, or plain water. As to wine, it being the custom, where he was, for the company to invite each other to drink in turn out of the same cup, he used sometimes to sip a little of it, to avoid appearing to shrink from it altogether, and to habituate himself to the common practice. For his eating he has been accustomed to prefer beef and salt meats, and household bread thoroughly fermented, to those articles of diet which are commonly regarded as delicacies. But he does not shrink from things that impart an innocent pleasure, even of a bodily kind, and has always a good

---

1 *according to ... about* Things such as the proper appearance of the toga. (See Ovid, *De arte Amandi*, book 1, 514.)

appetite for milk-puddings and for fruit, and eats a dish of eggs with the greatest relish.

His voice is neither loud nor excessively low, but of a penetrating tone. It has nothing in it melodious or soft, but is simply suitable for speech, as he does not seem to have any natural talent for singing, though he takes pleasure in music of every kind. His articulation is wonderfully distinct, being equally free from hurry and from hesitation.

He likes to be dressed simply, and does not wear silk, or purple, or gold chains, except when it is not allowable to dispense with them. He cares marvelously little for those formalities, which with ordinary people are the test of politeness; and as he does not exact these ceremonies from others, so he is not scrupulous in observing them himself, either on occasions of meeting or at entertainments, though he understands how to use them, if he thinks proper to do so; but he holds it to be effeminate and unworthy of a man to waste much of his time on such trifles.

He was formerly rather disinclined to a court life and to any intimacy with princes, having always special hatred of tyranny and a great fancy for equality; whereas you will scarcely find any court so well-ordered, as not to have much bustle and ambition and pretence and luxury, or to be free from tyranny in some form or other. He could not even be tempted to Henry the Eighth's court without great trouble, although nothing could be desired more courteous or less exacting than this Prince. He is naturally fond of liberty and leisure; but as he enjoys a holiday when he has it, so whenever business requires it, no one is more vigilant or more patient.

He seems to be born and made for friendship, of which he is the sincerest and most persistent devotee. Neither is he afraid of that multiplicity of friends, of which Hesiod disapproves. Accessible to every tender of intimacy, he is by no means fastidious in choosing his acquaintance, while he is most accommodating in keeping it on foot, and constant in retaining it. If he has fallen in with anyone whose faults he cannot cure, he finds some opportunity of parting with him, untying the knot of intimacy without tearing it; but when he has found any sincere friends, whose characters are suited to his own, he is so delighted with their society and conversation, that he seems to find in these the chief pleasure of life, having an absolute distaste for tennis and dice and cards, and the other games with which the mass of gentlemen beguile the tediousness of Time. It should be added that, while he is somewhat neglectful of his own interest, no one takes more pains in attending to the concerns of his friends. What more need I say? If anyone requires a perfect example of true friendship, it is in More that he will best find it.

In company his extraordinary kindness and sweetness of temper are such as to cheer the dullest spirit, and alleviate the annoyance of the most trying circumstances. From boyhood he was always so pleased with a joke, that it might seem that jesting was the main object of his life; but with all that, he did not go so far as buffoonery, nor had ever any inclination to bitterness. When quite a youth, he wrote farces and acted them. If a thing was facetiously said, even though it was aimed at himself, he was charmed with it, so much did he enjoy any witticism that had a flavour of subtlety or genius. This led to his amusing himself as a young man with epigrams, and taking great delight in Lucian. Indeed, it was he that suggested my writing the *Moria*, or Praise of Folly, which was much the same thing as setting a camel to dance.

There is nothing that occurs in human life, from which he does not seek to extract some pleasure, although the matter may be serious in itself. If he has to do with the learned and intelligent, he is delighted with their cleverness, if with unlearned or stupid people, he finds amusement in their folly. He is not offended even by professed clowns, as he adapts himself with marvellous dexterity to the tastes of all; while with ladies generally, and even with his wife, his conversation is made up of humour and playfulness. You would say it was a second Democritus,[1] or rather that Pythagorean philosopher,[2] who strolls in leisurely mood through the market-place, contemplating the turmoil of those who buy and sell. There is no one less guided by the opinion of the multitude, but on the other hand no one sticks more closely to common sense.

One of his amusements is in observing the forms, characters and instincts of different animals. Accordingly there is scarcely any kind of bird, that he does not keep about his residence, and the same of other animals not quite so common, as monkeys, foxes, ferrets, wea-

---

1   *Democritus* A pre-Socratic philosopher of Ancient Greece (c. 460-370 BCE).
2   *that Pythagorean philosopher* Socrates.

sels and the like. Beside these, if he meets with any strange object, imported from abroad or otherwise remarkable, he is most eager to buy it, and has his house so well supplied with these objects, that there is something in every room which catches your eye, as you enter it; and his own pleasure is renewed every time that he sees others interested.

When of a sentimental age, he was not a stranger to the emotions of love, but without loss of character, having no inclination to press his advantage, and being more attracted by a mutual liking than by any licentious object.

He had drunk deep of Good Letters from his earliest years; and when a young man, he applied himself to the study of Greek and of philosophy; but his father was so far from encouraging him in this pursuit, that he withdrew his allowance and almost disowned him, because he thought he was deserting his hereditary study, being himself an expert professor of English law. For remote as that profession is from true learning, those who become masters of it have the highest rank and reputation among their countrymen; and it is difficult to find any readier way to acquire fortune and honour. Indeed a considerable part of the nobility of that island has had its origin in this profession, in which it is said that no one can be perfect, unless he has toiled at it for many years. It was natural that in his younger days our friend's genius, born for better things, should shrink from this study; nevertheless, after he had had a taste of the learning of the Schools, he became so conversant with it, that there was no one more eagerly consulted by suitors; and the income that he made by it was not surpassed by any of those who did nothing else; such was the power and quickness of his intellect.

He also expended considerable labor in persuading the volumes of the orthodox fathers; and when scarcely more than a youth, he lectured publicly on the *De Civitate Dei*[1] of Augustine before a numerous audience, old men and priests not being ashamed to take a lesson in divinity from a young layman, and not at all sorry to have done so. Meantime he applied his whole mind to religion, having some thought of taking orders, for which he prepared himself by watchings and fastings and prayers and such like exercises; wherein he showed much more wisdom than the generality of the people who rashly engage in so arduous a profession without testing themselves

---

1 *De Civitate Dei* Of the City of God.

beforehand. And indeed there was no obstacle to his adopting this kind of life, except the fact, that he could not shake off his wish to marry. Accordingly he resolved to be a chaste husband rather than a licentious priest.

When he married, he chose a very young girl, a lady by birth, with her character still unformed, having been always kept in the country with her parents and sisters,—so that he was all the better able to fashion her according to his own habits. Under his direction she was instructed in learning and in every kind of Music, and had almost completely become just such a person as would have been a delightful companion for his whole life, if an early death had not carried her away. She had however borne him several children, of whom three girls, Margaret, Alice and Cecily, and one boy, John, are still living.

More did not however long remain single, but contrary to his friends' advice, a few months after his wife's death, he married a widow, more for the sake of the management of his household, than to please his own fancy, as she is no great beauty, nor yet young, *nec bella admodum nec puella*,[1] as he sometimes laughingly says, but a sharp and watchful housewife; with whom nevertheless he lives, on as sweet and pleasant terms as if she were as young and lovely as any one could desire; and scarcely any husband obtains from his wife by masterfulness and severity as much compliance as he does by blandishments and jests. Indeed, what more compliance could he have, when he has induced a woman who is already elderly, who is not naturally of a yielding character, and whose mind is occupied with business, to learn to play on the harp, the viol, the spinet and the flute, and to give up every day a prescribed time to practice? With similar kindness he rules his whole household, in which there are no tragic incidents, and no quarrels. If anything of the kind should be likely, he either calms it down, or applies a remedy at once. And in parting with any member of his household he has never acted in a hostile spirit, or treated him as an enemy. Indeed his house seems to have a sort of fatal felicity, no one having lived in it without being advanced to higher fortune, no inmate having ever had a stain upon his character.

It would be difficult to find any one living on such terms with a mother as he does with his step-mother. For his father had brought in one stepmother after another; and he has been as affectionate with

---

1   *nec ... puella*   Neither a very young nor a beautiful girl.

each of them as with a mother. He has lately introduced a third, and More swears that he never saw anything better. His affection for his parents, children and sisters is such, that he neither wearies them with his love, nor ever fails in any kindly attention.

His character is entirely free from any touch of avarice. He has set aside out of his property what he thinks sufficient for his children, and spends the rest in a liberal fashion. When he was still dependent on his profession, he gave every client true and friendly counsel with an eye to their advantage rather than his own, generally advising them, that the cheapest thing they could do was to come to terms with their opponents. If he could not persuade them to do this, he pointed out how they might go to law at least expense; for there are some people whose character leads them to delight in litigation.

In the city of London, where he was born, he acted for some years as judge in civil causes. This office, which is by no means burdensome,—inasmuch as the Court sits only on Thursdays before dinner,—is considered highly honorable; and no judge ever disposed of more suits, or conducted himself with more perfect integrity. In most cases he remitted the fees which are due from the litigants, the practice being for the plaintiff to deposit three groats before the hearing, and the defendant a like sum, and no more being allowed to be exacted. By such conduct he made himself extremely popular in the city.

He had made up his mind to be contented with this position, which was sufficiently dignified without being exposed to serious dangers. He has been thrust more than once into an embassy, in the conduct of which he has shown great ability; and King Henry in consequence would never rest until he dragged him into his court. 'Dragged him,' I say, and with reason; for no one was ever more ambitious of being admitted into a court, than he was anxious to escape it. But as this excellent monarch was resolved to pack his household with learned, serious, intelligent and honest men, he especially insisted upon having More among them,—with whom he is on such terms of intimacy that he cannot bear to let him go. If serious affairs are in hand, no one gives wiser counsel; if it pleases the King to relax his mind with agreeable conversation, no man is better company. Difficult questions are often arising, which require a grave and prudent judge; and these questions are resolved by More in such a way, that both sides are satisfied. And yet no one has ever induced him to accept a present. What a blessing it would be for the world, if magistrates like More were everywhere put in office by sovereigns!

Meantime there is no assumption of superiority. In the midst of so great a pressure of business he remembers his humble friends; and from time to time he returns to his beloved studies. Whatever authority he derives from his rank, and whatever influence he enjoys by the favour of a powerful sovereign, are employed in the service of the public, or in that of his friends. It has always been part of his character to be most obliging to every body, and marvellously ready with his sympathy; and this disposition is more conspicuous than ever, now that his power of doing good is greater. Some he relieves with money, some he protects by his authority, some he promotes by his recommendation, while those whom he cannot otherwise assist are benefited by his advice. No one is sent away in distress, and you might call him the general patron of all poor people. He counts it a great gain to himself, if he has relieved some oppressed person, made the path clear for one that was in difficulties, or brought back into favour one that was in disgrace. No man more readily confers a benefit, no man expects less in return. And successful as he is in so many ways,—while success is generally accompanied by self-conceit,—I have never seen any mortal being more free from this failing.

I now propose to turn to the subject of those studies which have been the chief means of bringing More and me together. In his first youth his principal literary exercises were in verse. He afterwards wrestled for a long time to make his prose more smooth; practising his pen in every kind of writing in order to form that style, the character of which there is no occasion for me to recall, especially to you, who have his books always in your hands. He took the greatest pleasure in declamations, choosing some disputable subject, as involving a keener exercise of mind. Hence, while still a youth, he attempted a dialogue, in which he carried the defence of Plato's community even to the matter of wives![1] He wrote an answer to Lucian's *Tyrannicide,* in which argument it was his wish to have me for a rival, in order to test his own proficiency in this kind of writing.

---

1 *Plato's ... wives* In Plato's *Republic*, Socrates makes the controversial claim that the guardian class of his ideal state would have no monogamous marriage; but rather the men would hold all the wives, and the women hold all the husbands, in common.

He published his *Utopia* for the purpose of showing, what are the things that occasion mischief in commonwealths; having the English constitution especially in view, which he so thoroughly knows and understands. He had written the second book at his leisure, and afterwards, when he found it was required, added the first off-hand. Hence there is some inequality in the style.

It would be difficult to find any one more successful in speaking *ex tempore*,[1] the happiest thoughts being attended by the happiest language; while a mind that catches and anticipates all that passes, and a ready memory, having everything as it were in stock, promptly supply whatever the time, or the occasion, demands. In disputations nothing can be imagined more acute, so that the most eminent theologians often find their match, when he meets them on their own ground. Hence John Colet, a man of keen and exact judgment, is wont to say in familiar conversation, that England has only one genius, whereas that island abounds in distinguished intellects.

However averse he may be from all superstition, he is a steady adherent of true piety; having regular hours for his prayers, which are not uttered by rote, but from the heart. He talks with his friends about a future life in such a way as to make you feel that he believes what he says, and does not speak without the best hope. Such is More, even at Court; and there are still people who think that Christians are only to be found in monasteries! Such are the persons, whom a wise King admits into his household, and into his chamber; and not only admits, but invites, nay, compels them to come in. These he has by him as the constant witnesses and judges of his life,—as his advisers and travelling companions. By these he rejoices to be accompanied, rather than by dissolute young men or by fops, or even by decorated grandees, or by crafty ministers, of whom one would lure him to silly amusements, another would incite him to tyranny, and a third would suggest some fresh schemes for plundering his people. If you had lived at this Court, you would, I am sure, give a new description of Court life, and cease to be Misaulos;[2] though you too live with such a prince, that you cannot wish for a better, and have some companions like Stromer and Copp, whose sympathies are on the right side. But what is that small number compared with such a swarm of distin-

---

1   *ex tempore* I.e., spontaneously.
2   *Misaulos* Literally, one who hates flutes; in this context, one who hates court life.

guished men as Mountjoy, Linacre, Pace, Colet, Stokesley, Latimer, More, Tunstall, Clerk, and others like them, any one of whose names signifies at once a world of virtues and accomplishments? However, I have no mean hope, that Albert, who is at this time the one ornament of our Germany, will attach to his household a multitude of persons like himself, and set a notable example to other princes; so that they may exert themselves in their own circles to do the like.

You have now before you an ill-drawn portrait, by a poor artist, of an excellent original! You will be still less pleased with the portrait, if you come to have a closer acquaintance with More himself. But meantime I have made sure of this, that you will not be able to charge me with neglecting your command, nor continue to find fault with the shortness of my letters; though even this one has not seemed too long to me in writing it, and will not, I am confident, appear prolix to you, as you read it; our More's sweetness will secure that....

from Plato, *Republic* (c. 380 BCE) [1]

> By More's own admission, Plato's *Republic* provides a significant source of inspiration for *Utopia*. Some of the ideas that influenced More are evident in this selection, in which Socrates and his interlocutors discuss the governors of their imagined ideal republic.

a. from Book 3

SOCRATES. ... The next question is: Who are to be our rulers? First, the elder must rule the younger; and the best of the elders will be the best guardians. Now they will be the best who love their subjects most, and think that they have a common interest with them in the welfare of the state. These we must select; but they must be watched at every epoch of life to see whether they have retained the same opinions and held out against force and enchantment. For time and persuasion and the love of pleasure may enchant a man into a change of purpose, and the force of grief and pain may compel him. And therefore our guardians must be men who have been tried by many tests, like gold in the refiner's fire, and have been passed first

---

1   *Republic*   Translated by Benjamin Jowett, 1871; in some cases, the English has been modernized for publication in this volume.

through danger, then through pleasure, and at every age have come out of such trials victorious and without stain, in full command of themselves and their principles; having all their faculties in harmonious exercise for their country's good. These shall receive the highest honours both in life and death. (It would perhaps be better to confine the term "guardians" to this select class: the younger men may be called "auxiliaries.")

And now for one magnificent lie, in the belief of which I wish that we could train our own rulers! At any rate, let us make the attempt with the rest of the world. What I am going to tell is only another version of the legend of Cadmus, but our unbelieving generation will be slow to accept such a story. The tale must be imparted, first to the rulers, then to the soldiers, lastly to the people. We will inform them that their youth was a dream, and that during the time when they seemed to be undergoing their education they were really being fashioned in the earth, who sent them up when they were ready; and that they must protect and cherish her whose children they are, and regard each other as brothers and sisters.

ADEIMANTUS. I do not wonder at your being ashamed to propound such a fiction.

SOCRATES. There is more besides. These brothers and sisters have different natures, and some of them God framed to rule, whom he fashioned of gold; others he made of silver, to be auxiliaries; others again to be farmers and craftsmen, and these were formed by him of brass and iron. But as they are all sprung from a common stock, a golden parent may have a silver son, or a silver parent a golden son, and then there must be a change of rank. The son of the rich must descend, and the child of the artisan rise, in the social scale; for an oracle says that "the State will come to an end if governed by a man of brass or iron." Will our citizens ever believe all this?

ADEIMANTUS. Not in the present generation, but in the next, perhaps, yes.

SOCRATES. Now let these heroes go forth under the command of their rulers, and pitch their camp in a high place, which will be safe against enemies from without, and likewise against insurrections from within. There let them sacrifice and set up their tents; for they are to be soldiers and not shopkeepers, the watchdogs and guardians of the sheep; and luxury and avarice will turn them into wolves and tyrants. Their habits and their dwellings should correspond to their education. They should have no property; their pay should only meet their expenses; and they should have common meals. Gold and silver we will tell them that they have from God, and this divine gift in their souls they must not alloy with that earthly dross which passes under the name of gold. Only they of all the citizens may not touch it, or be under the same roof with it, or drink from it; it is the accursed thing. Should they ever acquire houses or lands or money of their own, they will become householders and tradesmen instead of guardians, enemies and tyrants instead of helpers, and the hour of ruin, both to themselves and the rest of the State, will be at hand.

b. from Book 4

ADEIMANTUS. Suppose a person to argue, Socrates, that you make your citizens miserable, and this by their own free-will; they are the lords of the city, and yet instead of having, like other men, lands and houses and money of their own, they live as mercenaries and are always mounting guard.

SOCRATES. You may add that they receive no pay but only their food, and have no money to spend on a journey or a mistress.

ADEIMANTUS. Well, and what answer do you give?

SOCRATES. My answer is that our guardians may or may not be the happiest of men—although I should not be surprised to find in the long-run that they were—but this is not the aim of our constitution, which was designed for the good of the whole and not of any one part. If I went to a sculptor and blamed him for having painted the eye, which is the noblest feature of the face, not purple but black, he would reply: "The eye must be an eye, and you should look at the statue as a whole."

Now I can well imagine a fool's paradise, in which everybody is eating and drinking, clothed in purple and fine linen, and potters lie on sofas and have their wheel at hand, that they may work a little when they please; and cobblers and all the other classes of a State lose their distinctive character. And a State may get on without cobblers; but when the guardians degenerate into mere companions in leisure, then the ruin is complete. Remember that we are not talking of peasants keeping holiday, but of a State in which every man is expected to do his own work. The happiness resides not in this or that class, but in the State as a whole.

I would like to add that a middle condition is best for artisans; they should have money enough to buy tools, and not enough to be independent of business. And will not the same condition be best for our citizens? If they are poor, they will be mean; if rich, luxurious and lazy; and in neither case contented.

ADEIMANTUS. But then how will our poor city be able to go to war against an enemy who has money?

SOCRATES. There may be a difficulty in fighting against one enemy; against two there will be none. In the first place, the contest will be carried on by trained warriors against well-to-do citizens, and is not a regular athlete an easy match for two stout opponents at least? Suppose also, that before engaging we send ambassadors to one of the two cities, saying, "Silver and gold we have not; do you help us and take our share of the spoil?" Who would fight against the lean, wiry dogs, when they might join with them in preying upon the fatted sheep?

from Lucian, *Saturnalian Letters*[1]

Lucian of Samosata (c. 125-after 180 CE) was an Assyrian rhetorician known for his satirical wit. More and Erasmus worked together on a translation of Lucian's work that was very popular during More's life-time—it was reprinted more often even than *Utopia*. Parallels between Lucian's thought and More's are evident in the following excerpts from the *Saturnalian Letters*, which primarily discuss class relations and the distribution of wealth. The letters begin with a complaint to the god Cronus, also known as Saturn; the festival Lucian refers to is Saturna-lia, a week-long celebration involving feasting and playful role revers-als between the rich and poor.

I to Cronus, Greeting.

I have written to you before telling you of my condition, how pov-erty was likely to exclude me from the festival you have proclaimed. I remember observing how unreasonable it was that some of us should be in the lap of wealth and luxury, and never give a share of their good

---

1 *Saturnalian Letters* Translated by H.W. Fowler and F.G. Fowler, 1905.

things to the poor, while others are dying of hunger with your holy season just upon them. But as you did not answer, I thought I might as well refresh your memory. Dear good Cronus, you ought really to remove this inequality and pool all the good things before telling us to make merry. The world is peopled with camels and ants now, nothing between the two. Or, to put it another way, kindly imagine an actor, with one foot mounted on the tragic stilt and the other bare; if he walks like that, he must be a giant or a dwarf according to the leg he stands on; our lives are about as equal as his heights. Those who are taken on by manager Fortune and supplied with stilts come the hero over us, while the rest pad it on the ground, though you may take my word for it we could rant and stalk with the best of them if we were given the same chance.

Now the poets inform me that in the old days when you were king[1] it was otherwise with men; earth bestowed her gifts upon them unsown and unploughed, every man's table was spread automatically, rivers ran wine and milk and honey. Most wonderful of all, the men themselves were gold, and poverty never came near them. As for us, we can hardly pass for lead; some yet meaner material must be found. In the sweat of our face the most of us eat bread. Poverty, distress, and helplessness, sighs and lamentations and pinings for what is not, such is the staple of man's life, the poor man's at least. All which, believe me, would be much less painful to us, if there were not the felicity of the rich to emphasize it. They have their chests of gold and silver, their stored wardrobes, their slaves and carriages and house property and farms, and, not content with keeping to themselves their super-fluity in all these, they will scarce fling a glance to the generality of us.

Ah, Cronus, there is the sting that rankles beyond endurance—that one should loll on cloth of finest purple, overload his stomach with all delicacies, and keep perpetual feast with guests to wish him joy, while I and my like dream over the problematic acquisition of a sixpence to provide us a loaf white or brown, and send us to bed with a smack of cress or thyme or onion in our mouths. Now, good Cronus, either reform this altogether and feed us alike, or at the least induce the rich not to enjoy their good things alone; from their bush-els of gold let them scatter a poor pint among us; the raiment that they would never feel the loss of though the moth were to consume

---

1   *old days ... king*   Cronus ruled during the mythological Golden Age.

it utterly, seeing that in any case it must perish by mere lapse of time, let them devote to covering our nakedness rather than to propagating mildew in their chests and drawers....

Cronus to his well-beloved me, Greeting.

My good man, why this absurdity of writing to me about the state of the world, and advising redistribution of property? It is none of my business; the present ruler must see to that. It is an odd thing you should be the only person unaware that I have long abdicated;[1] my sons now administer various departments, of which the one that concerns you is mainly in the hands of Zeus; my own charge is confined to draughts and merry-making, song and good cheer, and that for one week only. As for the weightier matters you speak of, removal of inequalities and reducing of all men to one level of poverty or riches, Zeus must do your business for you....

Speaking generally, however, I must tell you that you are all in error; it is quite a misconception to imagine the rich in perfect bliss; they have no monopoly of life's pleasures because they can eat expensive food, drink too much good wine, revel in beauty, and go in soft raiment. You have no idea of how it works out. The resulting anxieties are very considerable. A ceaseless watch must be kept, or stewards will be lazy and dishonest, wine go sour, and grain be weeviled; the burglar will be off with the rich man's plate; agitators will persuade the people that he is meditating a *coup d'état*. And these are but a minute fraction of their troubles; if you could know their apprehensions and cares, you would think riches a thing to be avoided at all costs....

You made a great fuss in your letter about *their* gorging on boar's head and pastry while *your* festival consists of a mouthful of cress or thyme or onion. Now, what are the facts? As to the immediate sensation, on the palate, there is little to choose between the two diets—not much to complain of in either; but with the after effects it is quite otherwise. *You* get up next morning without either the headache the rich man's wine leaves behind, or the disgusting queasiness that results from his surfeit of food. To these effects he adds those of nights given to lust and debauchery, and as likely as not reaps the fruit of his luxury in consumption, pneumonia, or dropsy. It is quite a difficult

---

1   *I have ... abdicated*   In myth, Cronus was overthrown by his sons and succeeded by Zeus.

matter to find a rich man who is not deathly pale; most of them by the time they are old men use eight legs belonging to other people instead of their own two; they are gold without and rags within, like the stage hero's robes. No fish dinners for you, I admit; you hardly know what fish tastes like; but then observe, no gout or pneumonia either, nor other ailments due to other excesses. Apart from that, though, the rich themselves do not enjoy their daily over-indulgence in these things; you may see them as eager, and more, for a dinner of herbs as ever you are for game.

... [T]here are numberless things, in fact, that you know nothing about; you only see their gold and purple, or catch sight of them behind their high-steppers, and open your mouths and abase yourselves before them. If you left them severely alone, if you did not turn to stare at their silver-plated carriages, if you did not while they were talking eye their emerald rings, or finger their clothes and admire the fineness of the texture, if you let them keep their riches to themselves, in short, I can assure you they would seek you out and implore the favour of your company; you see, they must show you their couches and tables and goblets, the sole good of which is in the being known to possess them.

You will find that most of their acquisitions are made for you; they are not for their own use, but for your astonishment. I am one that knows both lives, and I write this for your consolation. You should keep the feast with the thought in your minds that both parties will soon leave this earthly scene, they resigning their wealth, and you your poverty....

from Acts of the Apostles, 4.32–5.11

In *Utopia*, More refers to the communal sharing of goods as a Christian practice. This practice as undertaken by the apostles and their early converts is described in the following biblical passage.

And the multitude of them that believed were of one heart and of one soul: neither said any of them that ought of the things which he possessed was his own; but they had all things common. And with great power gave the apostles witness of the resurrection of the Lord Jesus: and great grace was upon them all.

Neither was there any among them that lacked: for as many as were possessors of lands or houses sold them, and brought the prices of the things that were sold, and laid them down at the apostles' feet: and distribution was made unto every man according as he had need.

And Joses, who by the apostles was surnamed Barnabas, (which is, being interpreted, The son of consolation), a Levite, and of the country of Cyprus, having land, sold it, and brought the money, and laid it at the apostles' feet.

But a certain man named Ananias, with Sapphira his wife, sold a possession, and kept back part of the price, his wife also being privy to it, and brought a certain part, and laid it at the apostles' feet.

But Peter said, Ananias, why hath Satan filled thine heart to lie to the Holy Ghost, and to keep back part of the price of the land? While it remained, was it not thine own? And after it was sold, was it not in thine own power? Why hast thou conceived this thing in thine heart? Thou hast not lied unto men, but unto God.

And Ananias hearing these words fell down, and gave up the ghost: and great fear came on all them that heard these things. And the young men arose, wound him up, and carried him out, and buried him.

And it was about the space of three hours after, when his wife, not knowing what was done, came in.

And Peter answered unto her, Tell me whether ye sold the land for so much? And she said, Yea, for so much.

Then Peter said unto her, How is it that ye have agreed together to tempt the Spirit of the Lord? Behold, the feet of them which have buried thy husband are at the door, and shall carry thee out.

Then fell she down straightway at his feet, and yielded up the ghost: and the young men came in, and found her dead, and, carrying her forth, buried her by her husband. And great fear came upon all the church, and upon as many as heard these things.